I0551497

I WALKED WITH JESUS

New Testament Stories of Faith and Healing

From the Least of These

Books by Kathryn Elizabeth Jones

A River of Stones

Parable Series

> Conquering Your Goliaths: A Parable of the Five Stones
>
> Conquering Your Goliaths: Guidebook
>
> The Feast: A Parable of the Ring
>
> The Gift: A Parable of the Key
>
> The Parables of Virginia Bean

Heaven 24/7 - Living in the Light

Marketing Your Book on a Budget

Susan Cramer Mysteries

> Scrambled   Hard Boiled
>
> Sunny Side-Up   Over Easy

Brianne James Mysteries

> Tie Died   Buckled Inn

Mooseberry Mooseberry Gooseberry Pie

The Space Adventures of Aaden Prescott

> LightShade   LightDescending

Enlightened - My Personal Journey with Christ Through Scripture Journaling

The Human Bean

I Walked With Jesus – New Testament Stories of Faith & Healing From the Least of These

I WALKED WITH JESUS

New Testament Stories of Faith and Healing
From the Least of These

Kathryn Elizabeth Jones

www.ideacreationspress.com

 Idea Creations Press
www.ideacreationspress.com

Copyright © Kathryn Elizabeth Jones, 2021.

All rights reserved. No part of this book may be reproduced or transmitted in any form or by any means, electronic or mechanical, including photocopying, recording, or by an information storage and retrieval system, without permission in writing from the author.

This is not an official publication of The Church of Jesus Christ of Latter-Day Saints. The opinions and views expressed herein belong solely to the author.

978-1948804226

LIBRARY OF CONGRESS CATALOGING-IN-PUBLICATION DATA

Jones, Kathryn Elizabeth, author
I Walked With Jesus / By Kathryn Elizabeth Jones
First trade paperback original edition. | Salt Lake City: Idea Creations Press, 2021.
ISBN 978-1948804226 | LCCN 2021945381
Jesus Christ / Inspirational | Spirituality / | BISAC: RELIGION / Christian Living / Spiritual Growth

Printed in the U. S. A

Jesus Christ – Heinrich Hofmann, 1884

"He came unto his own, and his own received him not. But as many as received him, to them gave He power to become the sons [and daughters] of God, even to them that believe on his name" (John 1:11-12).

Author's Note:

I have taken a few liberties with these New Testament stories. For most of them, a name was not attached to the story. For all, I had to come up with a backstory to honor the faith promoting and healing experiences with the Savior. I have done my best to keep all historical facts accurate; and, at the same time, allow my heart the freedom to create the story I felt needed to be told.

I thank many historians who have gathered the facts about the time of Christ and placed them within easy access – thank heavens for computers – saving me hours of research time.

Some dialogue used in I Walked With Jesus has come directly from the Bible. This dialogue has been interwoven with dialogue I have imagined Christ or the least of these to have said. For questions about what is from the scriptures themselves, please refer to the scriptural reference heading each chapter.

I am grateful for the scriptures*; without them, none of these stories could have been written. I thank the Lord who is also first in my life. For all He has shown me and continues to teach me, I will be forever grateful.

*With two exceptions (Doctrine and Covenants, 7: 1-3; and JST John 4:26), all scripture references have been taken from the King James Bible.

Have you ever considered yourself
as one of the least of these?

Contents

Jesus Christ and Nicodemus - Alexandre Bida, 1874

The Rabbi
John 3

Since the first time he'd spoken with the Rabbi of Galilee, Nicodemus' heart had burned. There was something about the man called Jesus of Nazareth that made him want to change his heart, maybe even his life.

His home was large with many rooms, but he'd chosen to visit with the Rabbi outdoors, near the great well where places for sitting in the cooler evening air were appreciated. Jesus must come at night, when peering eyes slept, and when his leadership duties were not so pressing. If his neighbors saw his visitor, he could merely remind them that it was the law to study at night – besides, it was expected. He need not worry about his place in the social and political arena.

Still, as Jesus entered, Nicodemus' heart skipped more than one beat. He was curious to know the truth, but he was also deeply afraid of what he would hear. Jesus was a great teacher, but he was not a prophet.

Or was he?

Because it was dark the torches had been lit. The dripping of water within the well where they spoke reminded Nicodemus of the cleansing of his soul – what he feared the most.

The sound of Jesus' sandals padded toward him. He stopped and sat. Nicodemus followed.

"A drink?" he asked.

The Rabbi shook his head.

"Well, then, I will begin," he offered.

The wind was blowing softly and easily, and Nicodemus was glad he'd chosen the location he had. But where should he start? He'd gone over the conversation a million times, and now that Jesus of Nazareth was here, he was at a loss.

The man was looking intently at him, so Nicodemus began:

"Rabbi, we know that thou art a teacher come from God: for no man can do these miracles that thou doest, except God be with him."

Jesus smiled. "Verily, verily, I say unto thee, except a man be born again, he cannot see the kingdom of God."

Born... again? Nicodemus thought. "How can a man be born when he is old? Can he enter the second time into his mother's womb, and be born?" he asked.

Even in the dim light, he could see that Jesus' eyes were blue, the color of the sea of Galilee where he sometimes walked to clear his head.

"Verily, verily, I say unto thee, except a man be born of water and of the Spirit, he cannot enter into the kingdom of God."

Children were born of the water from their mother's womb. And there was a spirit that dwelt inside every man.

"That which is born of the flesh is flesh; and that which is born of the Spirit is spirit. Marvel not that I said unto thee, Ye must be born again. The wind bloweth where it listeth, and thou hearest the sound thereof but canst not tell whence it cometh, and whither it goeth: so is every one that is born of the Spirit."

12

"How can these things be?" Nicodemus asked, taking a sip of the wine he had poured for himself. "Art thou a master of Israel, and knowest not these things? Verily, verily, I say unto thee, we speak that we do know, and testify that we have seen; and ye receive not our witness. I have told you of earthly things, and ye believe not, how shall ye believe, if I tell you of heavenly things?"

For a moment Nicodemus thought of the wind in the trees, but the thought forming in his head escaped him as Jesus continued:

"And no man hath ascended up to heaven, but he that came down from heaven, even the Son of man which is in heaven. And as Moses lifted up the serpent in the wilderness, even so must the Son of man be lifted up: That whosoever believeth in him should not perish, but have eternal life."

Nicodemus knew of Moses and the serpent he raised up. He knew the law of Moses and had lived it since he was young. But who would come down from heaven and be lifted up? Was Jesus speaking of himself?

"For God so loved the world, that he gave his only begotten Son, that whosover believeth in him should not perish, but have everlasting life."

A trickling of warmth found his soul.

"For God sent not his Son into the world to condemn the world; but that the world through him might be saved. He that believeth on him is not condemned: but he that believeth not is condemned already, because he hath not believed in the name of the only begotten Son of God."

Did he believe? Was this truly the Son of God?

"And this is the condemnation," the teacher continued, "that light is come into the world, and men loved darkness rather than light, because their deeds were evil."

Was Jesus saying *his* deeds were evil?

"For every one that doeth evil hateth the light, neither cometh to the light, lest his deeds should be reproved."

Suddenly, Nicodemus was thinking of his sins. He had many, but so did others in his position. In his duties as a ruler of the Jews and a member of the Sanhedrin, he must set an example of strength.

"But he that doeth truth cometh to the light, that his deeds may be manifest, that they are wrought in God."

Nicodemus took another sip of wine, but he could not meet the eyes of the teacher. Both were silent, and as Nicodemus listened to the wind through the trees, and the dripping sound of the water in his well, he was anxious to go inside to his family.

Jesus stood.

"Follow me," he said.

They were at the front of his house before Jesus spoke again. "Follow me. Learn of me."

The wind brushing against Nicodemus' face, and the rustle of leaves above his head seemed to speak words of comfort. Could he do it? Could he leave his home, his profession? He had felt something warm prick at his chest. Could he deny now what he thought to be true?

Tears glistened. "I believe thy words are true," he said.

"Then, come, follow me."

The repeated entreaty was followed by a smile and a touch of a hand to his shoulder.

"When?"

"Tomorrow. We leave tomorrow."

Nicodemus breathed in slowly and as his breath escaped his lips, he looked into Jesus' eyes. They were still looking at him, watching him lovingly. He had never before seen such eyes.

"I don't... know," he stumbled. "You say you are leaving tomorrow?"

"Tomorrow. Will you be there?"

With all of his heart, Nicodemus wanted to say yes, but the words he wanted to say stuck in his throat. "I don't know..." he began.

"Think about it?" Jesus offered.

"I will," he answered.

A sob escaped Nicodemus' lips. "Master?" he asked. "If I don't come, will you yet love me?"

Of all the things he could have said, these words were the hardest. He knew that tomorrow he would not come. He would eat, he would go about his duties, he would walk the grounds of his beautiful home and the synagogue, but Jesus would travel without him.

Still, watching the man who some believed was God, there was no question in those heavenly eyes about his answer.

Christus und die Samariterin am Brunnen - Angelika Kauffmann, 1796

Woman at the Well
John 4

From the time she was small, Susanna, a Samaritan, felt hidden and inconsequential. She was a girl, a girl who would grow into a woman, but, like every other woman living in Samaria, she must be content with what she had.

With the proposal of marriage, by a young man well-liked in the city, came a sudden spark of acknowledgment, which pleased her. Like a candle lit in a darkened room, there was hope. Perhaps she wasn't as unseen as she thought. Perhaps her life would mean something after all.

As Tobias was in love with her, it was his duty to approach his parents, who would then approach her parents for consent. She did not know of the request at first but felt honored nonetheless. It was the way of Samaritan marriage. She would be expected to speak up, decline the offer if desired, or say yes. She accepted his proposal.

The betrothal ceremony followed soon thereafter. It happened in her home. She'd chosen a guardian – a priest from the family – to consent to their union. The ceremony to sustain the bond of their future together was given on her behalf.

She was thirteen.

Tobias, also a Samaritan, was a young man of seventeen – her cousin. He spoke to her little after their betrothal, preferring his friends, it seemed, to her company. Still, she would marry well. And she was happy at the outset, spending many hours with her mother learning how to cook, clean, and take care of other married life expectations.

By the time he was eighteen, and she, fourteen, they were married. There was a week of rejoicing and the gathering of loved ones before the four days of celebration, including multiple feasts, music, and a reading from the life of Rebekah from the Bible. But Susanna's favorite remembrance came on the third day, as the wearing of red clothing symbolized her virginity. She believed in God and his great love for her and was grateful she'd kept herself clean.

On the fourth day, the day of her marriage, the "Song of the Red Sea", was sung with the accompaniment of tambourines. Dancing followed, filling her with good thoughts. Tobias looked on her fondly, and she knew married life as Tobias's wife would bring her happiness.

By the time she was sixteen, their first child was born. It had taken some time, but finally, the blessings of God had come to her.

A girl. She was sweet and small and ignored by him. A son was what he wanted. Only a son.

But Susanna loved little Zillah. She was the only joy she had not including the moments she listened to the words of the Torah in the synagogue.

Friends came and went, but did not stay. There were always strict rules about how long they could visit, when, without warning, her husband would walk into the room, and escort the friend out. This, she learned later, was the law of her husband, and not the law regarding a Samaritan wife.

There were angry words almost every day now, about things inconsequential to her, but important to him. She would vow again to do her duty, and remember the laws of the Torah.

When, during Niddah, she could not touch her husband or child, she sat alone, and ate alone, until the seven days of impurity had passed. She could not enter the synagogue and he must take care of tiny Zillah without her. She could not help even when Zillah cried.

After Niddah, she purified herself, washed all the clothes she'd been wearing during her convalescence, and cleaned the utensils in running water. She was never allowed friends – not even her mother, during this time. And while her mother always came in to help her, she was not allowed to be with her in the same room.

Such was the Law for all Samaritan women, though Susanna felt more invisible than ever before. The fondness she'd felt for her husband did not last. There was never love. He was not kind to her and spent time complaining about her faults when he might have played with little Zillah or taken her in his arms. Perhaps she could have lived the Law, taken care of her little family with joy, and lived contentedly seeing as the Torah always raised her spirits, but with an angry, unfeeling husband, she could not.

When the time came for divorce, her husband complaining that the fighting in their marriage had made his life unbearable – she was pregnant with their second child.

She made no mention of the child she carried in her womb but finding the money needed to feed her two children would be difficult – if not impossible.

There was a man, however, who knew of her condition and protected her confidence. In those short weeks after the divorce, he cared for her. They married. Ethan was solid, enduring, and faithful. After the birth of her son, Ethan told no one, and others merely assumed the child was his. He took care of her and assisted with the children during the forty days she was impure, in addition to the day of circumcision. As a carpenter, Ethan was skilled in furniture making, and the business flourished under his hand.

Jesse was a gift to them both. Their little son grew, and as the days passed, Jesse smiled as he watched his father in the woodshop. When her husband became ill, neither she nor any of the attending physicians, knew what it was. Was it some stomach ailment, some disease of the tissue? They were never sure. When he died, Zillah was seven, and Jesse was six.

Susanna mourned for her husband. Strong drink calmed her thoughts until she found she could not distinguish one day from another. She was neglecting her children. She loved them but the drink gave way to forgetfulness.

Marrying her third husband, Jason, allowed her to keep the children. She did not love him, but he had watched over her husband until the very end. He was a good father to her children. As a physician, they were well taken care of, moved into a larger dwelling, and for a time, were kind to one another.

When the drinking began again for Susanna, he left her.

For a time, she lived alone, and the children, now three of them, were removed. She would never see them again.

She hardly knew Silas, her fourth husband. He drank as she did, and his home was small, and not well-kept; her fault. She took to bed mostly, unless she was going to retrieve water at the well. But even that was difficult. People in the village stared at her, and when Silas died, for a time she lived alone.

Jesse, who surprisingly bore the name of her second child, took care of her after that. Susanna, for all of her faults, was still beautiful, or so others said of her. Jesse was an unkind man, and she did not love him. Though married, and though he often said he loved her, she did not return his affection. She knew she was being unkind, but she couldn't forget Ethan, the man who yet dwelt within her heart. She cried for her children and looked for opportunities to watch them in the marketplace, but she never approached them. She couldn't approach them. As a mother, she had failed them.

When Jesse divorced her, she knew she would never marry again. But she needed someone. The loneliness of her heart continued. She was with a man named Phillip, who would never be her husband. No one looked at her now, not even him. "You have grown ugly," he'd say. He'd hit her, and accuse her of using him for her pleasures. Still, it was better to be with someone than to be alone. She had enough to eat, and shelter to pass the days.

Afternoons, when no one else was around, and when it was breathtakingly too hot to be outside, she would gather her vessel, and make her way slowly to Jacob's Well. The well had never dried out for as long as she could remember; surely, the water would refresh many for years to come.

Susanna had walked the dusty path many times before. Though the walk wasn't long, the vessel would be heavy upon her return. She always dreaded the walk home.

Jacob's Well was located near the bottom of Mt. Gerizim. It was deep and wide. A long rope was needed so that she might reach the base of the well to retrieve the water. She used an animal-skin vessel to gather and then carry the water home. The vessel could never be left at the well for any reason; one would surely return to find that someone had taken it.

It was the middle of the day, and even then, she could hear the voices behind the whispering hands of the women. "Did you know she is not married?" "I heard she's gone through five husbands." "She disgusts me."

Once, when she was much younger, she'd overheard her first husband speaking to his father before entering the synagogue. They had spoken in heated terms about the destruction of the Samaritan temple by the Jews on Mt. Gerizim. She could feel the hate like a sharp blade against her belly, just as she felt it now.

Tears formed under Susanna's eyelids. She had heard these words, and more. And she would hear them until the day she died.

Brushing past the women, her eyes focused on the path ahead. No one would be at the well at this hour, and she would have some solitude. She did not look up. She knew the looks that would confront her, even if the words were unspoken. She would think of Ethan, solid and enduring Ethan, and her children as she remembered them. She would get to the well, and then she would reach for the rope, tie it to the vessel, and drop it into the depths of the water.

She was surprised as she approached the well. A man was sitting there, looking off in the direction of Mt. Ebal to the north. As she drew closer, she wondered if he was a Jew. His clothing was woven like that of the Jews.

She dropped the vessel to the bottom of the well and waited for the rope to end its descent. The man watched her but said nothing.

Her shawl clung to her skin from the day's warmth. Bringing up the vessel, she was ready to leave, when he asked, "Give me to drink."

She was stunned.

"How is it that thou, being a Jew, askest of me, which am a woman of Samaria? For the Jews have no dealing with the Samaritans."

Why was he speaking to her?

22

"If thou knewest the gift of God, and who it is that saith to thee, Give me to drink; thou wouldest have asked of him, and he would have given thee living water."

The man's hands were empty. As his eyes looked on her, a feeling different than the heat of the sun warmed her skin.

"Sir, thou hast nothing to draw with, and the well is deep: from whence then hast thou that living water?" She placed the vessel at her feet and looked at him. "Art thou greater than our father Jacob, which gave us the well, and drank thereof himself, and his children, and his cattle?"

"Whosoever drinketh of this water shall thirst again. But whosoever drinketh of the water that I shall give him shall never thirst; but the water that I shall give him shall be in him a well of water springing up into everlasting life."

She had heard these words before. At synagogue, when the day was spent listening and praying. She had also heard the same words as a child as she'd studied religious law in the home, learned to read and write and to respect kosher – what she and her future household would be able to eat, and what utensils they would be required to eat with.

"Sir, give me this water, that I thirst not, neither come hither to draw."

What a blessing it would be not to come out in the heat of the day, she thought.

"Go, call thy husband, and come hither."

"I have no husband." She peered down at the water she'd recently drawn.

"Thou hast well said, I have no husband: For thou hast had five husbands, and he whom thou now hast is not thy husband: in that saidest thou truly."

Ethan and his kind ways; his generous love for her, came briefly but powerfully into her mind.

"Sir, I perceive that thou art a prophet. Our fathers worshipped in this mountain; and ye say, that in Jerusalem is the place men ought to worship."

Susanna remembered from her lessons as a child the Jew's rejection of the Samaritans' offer to help in the reconstruction of the temple. In anger, they had halted the re-building of the Jew's temple, if only for a time. In retaliation, a Jewish high priest had destroyed the Samaritan temple on Mt. Gerizim. The hatred, even after 160 years, had not healed between them – and perhaps it never would.

"Woman, believe me, the hour cometh, when ye shall neither in this mountain nor yet in Jerusalem, worship the Father. Ye worship ye know not what: we know what we worship: for salvation is of the Jews. But the hour cometh, and now is, when the true worshippers shall worship the Father in spirit and in truth: for the Father seeketh such to worship him. For unto such hath God promised his Spirit. And they who worship him, must worship in spirit and in truth.

A warmth like the sun rising, caressed her shoulders and rushed to her fingertips.

"I know that Messias cometh, which is called Christ: when he is come, he will tell us all things."

"I that speak unto thee am he."

Something burned inside her. What was this thing she had almost forgotten?

He'd seen everything. Whom she'd married, the children she'd had, her weaknesses, her anguished heart seeking forgiveness. He knew her, every part of her. How was that possible if he hadn't been the Messiah?

Her heart pounded. She wanted to shout the words at the top of her voice! She wanted the others to know that she had seen the very Christ. Her children, yes, they had to know, and her parents, and Phillip. Everyone! Jesus, the Messiah loved her, and because he loved her, she could love them, all of them, even those who had hurt her.

Her life could begin again.

Looking into the heavens, she took her first step, and in moments had entered the village where she lived. She told everyone she knew, shouting the name of the Messiah to the rooftops. At home, she spoke with Phillip. He looked at her strangely, and she imagined he thought her deluded. And then he took her hand. It was the first time in months he'd offered such a gesture.

"Are you sure?" he asked, "are you sure you've spoken with Jesus?"

Tears glistened in her eyes. All she could do was nod.

He spoke with her into the night about his dreams of knowing Him, dreams she had never known of until now.

The next morning, she touched the vessel of water she'd left at the well.

Amazingly, it was still there. And it was full.

She brought the full pitcher to her shoulder. Looking beyond the well and to the mountains that she knew so well, a thought entered her mind – a thought she'd never had before. There were many seekers of truth searching for water that would never dry up, that would always be there as Christ had said. Her journey to share what she had learned had not ended at the well. His words had not stopped at her village. They had not ended upon her return to Phillip.

She wasn't alone today. It was early, and there were many at the well, mostly women and children filling their vessels that would be empty the following day. Sitting her vessel beside the well, she looked on them fondly. Some stared back, but there was no hissing, no speaking behind the hand with hateful words. Not today.

Susanna smiled over at them. "I have something to tell you." The slightest breeze caressed her cheek. She could not see Him, but He was there. "I have met the Messiah," she began.

I Walked With Jesus

The Woman with an Issue of Blood – James Tissot, 1886-1896

A Certain Woman
Mark 5

Anna, named Joanna at birth, was loved and raised by her parents until the time she was sixteen. Despite the fact she was ritually unclean and had to leave them, she knew one thing: God loved her.

Today she lived in a small house in Capernaum, a simple structure, with uneven, stone walls, and a roof of palm leaves. But, unlike her parents, who had much, Anna was content to live out her days alone and poor, remembering the words her father and mother had often spoken to her about God.

The town in which she lived was a busy place, filled with fishermen, farmers, and traders of goods. Not a day went by without noise, and Anna was sure this was a blessing. She could not always think of herself as she listened to the drama that others experienced nearby.

The narrow street in which she lived, was near the Sea of Galilee, a short distance from her parents, and just around the corner from the customs office where Matthew was employed as a tax collector. No one liked Matthew either, and they had become friends, especially since the days she'd come to live alone.

Three years previous, when the time reserved for childbearing had come to her, Anna's mother had invited many doctors to come and see her. She'd tried everything: herbs, a cleaner diet, sitting more and walking less; even repenting when she was pretty sure she'd done nothing wrong. She was conscious that her life was in line with God's teachings. Despite the pain, the inconvenience, and the pleading to God, the bleeding did not stop.

Her kind parents had hidden her uncleanliness for a long time, but on the morning of her fifteenth birthday, word got out. Perhaps someone had heard about her plague on the rooftop where her family spoke together on hot summer evenings, or maybe someone had overheard her speaking to her mother in the marketplace. She was sick all of the time, and weak too. Much of her time was spent in bed, and the little time she was up and about was short.

A year went by. No one came to visit, no one dared touch her or any member of the family, and her father's trade business was now in jeopardy. Her mother could no longer walk the streets without gossip meeting her ears.

Her parents spoke to her again. It was time to go. And she need not worry. Matthew would support her. They already had a small shelter chosen near him where she could be watched over and cared for.

She was sixteen.

She cried.

Her mother and father cried. Her baby brother wailed as he had always done since the moment he'd been born. They laughed. He knew nothing of what she would have to do now. And then they cried again as she left them.

Up the narrow street, the dark stone houses to the right and left of her seemed to glare their hatred of her. She knew it was not the houses themselves that stared, but the people watching within and on rooftops at the unclean girl as she passed.

Most of those on the street were men; soldiers who protected the frontier or backed up the tax collectors. They were mercenary soldiers – not Romans – but men recruited from Phrygia, Germany, and Gaul. They served under Herod Antipas, the king. They walked stoically, but closer to her, finding their distance as best as they could.

She could smell the fishermen even before she saw them, the stink on their cloaks parading before them like invisible dancers, the soothing sound of the Sea of Galilee lapping against the rocks, the gentle wind drying her tears. All was in commotion but the sea.

It would not be long now.

She turned the corner and another; the customs office in sight. The shelter, just north of Matthew's large home, beckoned. He'd built an extra room adjoining the customs office, and they would talk some, in the evenings when prying eyes and ears had lessened. He had promised it.

Anna carried only her bedding and her personal belongings; all else would be provided for her. She rapped on the door once and entered the one-room shelter when no one answered. It was day yet, and Matthew, or Levi as some called him, would still be about the tax business.

She removed her sandals as was the custom, even though the floor was dirt with an addition of lime to harden the surface. She had gotten used to much better in her home; the flagstones beneath her feet were cool and kept her feet clean and dry. Still, the place would suffice. The room was clean and unexpectedly cheerful. A water pot sat in the corner near the circle of stones for the fire and a blue cloth graced a small table – a hard color to produce and a costly one too. Two low stools surrounded it. So, he had remembered.

Above her, palm leaves created a ceiling. The walls were made of clay, similar to the walls at home, only rougher and darker. The room was surprisingly clean of acrid smells she'd heard some of the poorer class knew, and instead, a corner by a high window was filled with pots of red sea-side poppy blooms in soil – just enough for her to take care of and keep growing – she could reach them by stool.

She'd noticed a well out front as she'd passed by, one used by Matthew and his household she was sure, but one he had promised to share with her. He would bring the water by every morning on his way to the customs office; water that was drawn each morning by a woman named Sara who worked for him and came to the house daily to care for his animals and house.

His shelter wasn't large compared to some, but he made a good living taxing the people who hated him. She'd seen his house as a young girl and had been surprised then by its simplicity. Only four small rooms surrounded two open courtyards. Her family had one courtyard, but the simple, coarse walls were the same and the roof of earth and straw was just like the roof at home.

There was something about Matthew that had impressed her even then. His quiet, but loving way, and the tenderness in his eyes as he listened to her. He did like his money, but not to a fault. He'd never married and yet had a good life. When she and her family had come to visit that first time, and many more times after that before she was pronounced ritually unclean, he had always set aside his endeavors in favor of friends.

He'd told her more than once upon preparation, that he wanted her to be safe. He wasn't afraid for his own life, believing that Jesus taught a higher law; only what others might do or say if they knew where she was living. Public association in the regular sense with women who did not have the plague was frowned upon anyway; the literature was clear on the subject: "He that talks much with womankind, brings evil upon himself and neglects the study of the Law… (1)"

Still, Anna knew Matthew had faith that all would be well. She would be careful and only travel in the evening, and then, only for a short time.

There was a bed. She placed her blankets there, and a shelf in the wall to store her clothing. She readied everything, then slept on the single low couch provided. When she awoke, it was dark. She stood to light the oil and carried the lamp to the window. All the businesses had closed. There was a softness in the air and as Anna directed the glow of the lamp to the window, she heard a knock.

Opening the door, a crack, she asked, "Who is it?"

"Your friend from long ago," came the answer. "I have brought food."

She opened the door, quickly noticing the satchel he had over his back. Walking to the table, and moving a corner of the blue cloth, Matthew set down the items.

"I've brought you bread, dates, olives, and a little goat's milk. You do like goat's milk?"

"Yes, I still like milk."

He smiled over at her. "Does the place suit you?"

"Very well."

"Good. I will bring water in the morning. Do you have everything you need?"

"Thank you, yes."

He nodded his head. "I wish I could do more."

"That is something you and I both understand," Anna said. "I thank you for your thoughtfulness."

He nodded once more as Anna opened the door.

"Oh, I almost forgot." He smiled again, looking into her eyes. "Inside the front pocket, you will see a special gift from me."

"You didn't have –"

The words had barely escaped her lips and he was gone.

Shutting the door, she turned to the table. Walking to it and reaching for the satchel she pushed her hand into the outside pocket. Retrieving a handful of papers, she began to scan their contents. There were words there, words she had often heard her father speak about Jesus when he spoke in the synagogue as a young man. Even then, her father wondered if he was the Messiah. She folded them to her chest. It was as if, in the very words, she could feel the light of goodness contained therein. She retreated to the couch, and with the light still glowing, read the words he had copied for her.

"Let thy mercies come also unto me, O LORD, *even* thy salvation, according to thy word.

So shall I have wherewith to answer him that reproacheth me: for I trust in thy word".

"Remember the word unto thy servant, upon which thou hast caused me to hope.

This *is* my comfort in my affliction: for thy word hath quickened me. The proud have had me greatly in derision: *yet* have I not declined from thy law. I remembered thy judgments of old, O LORD; and have comforted myself".

"The proud have forged a lie against me: *but* I will keep thy precepts with *my* whole heart. Their heart is as fat as grease; *but* I delight in thy law. *It is* good for me that I have been afflicted; that I might learn thy statutes. The law of thy mouth *is* better unto me than thousands of gold and silver".

Anna turned her eyes from the text and looked around the room, the room her parents and Matthew had provided for her.

Pressing the words against her lips, she set them down, carried the lamp to her bed, and made preparations for sleep.

Morning came too soon. The commotion outside was already at an uproar, loud voices producing a warmth that would soon be with her by mid-day. Turning to the door she opened it only a crack to find the water jug already waiting for her. The smells of the city were before her – of fish cooking, the sounds of people walking the streets, the road littered with unnecessary castoffs from the day before. She retrieved the jug gladly, shut the door, and carried it to the table.

She would need to bathe, but not now, not in the way she would have liked. But the water would do her soul good as well as her body, and the rags she now produced from the shelf where she kept her clothes would serve more than one use. This was another task not easily given to another, and so she had told him that evenings would work best – even though it was dangerous to be out at night. She would do all of her cleaning then as best she could when many would be asleep.

She would go by the way of the sea when she had the opportunity to do so. Until then, she would gather the bedding, the rags, and the needful things, and place them in a bag well hidden from view. If anyone happened by, if they saw her at any time, they would think her a lone woman, perhaps a widow or an unfortunate unmarried woman. She would speak little to them, keep to herself as counseled by Matthew and her parents, and enjoy what she did have.

Love. Truth. Food. Shelter.

It was enough.

But twelve years was a long time to be alone, even with occasional visits from Matthew, and the word of God he constantly delivered to her in her affliction. But he was a good man, and, as promised by her parents as well as by himself, he took care of her.

On his weekly visits, Matthew would tell her what her family was doing, he'd share with her their struggles and joys, and often, letters came from her mother or father reminding her of the goodness of God.

True, some nearby knew of her existence, but they didn't know where she had come from and she never said, although a few through the years might have wondered. She never met anyone formally, choosing to keep the door closed if they knocked or drew near the window. She knew of her uncleanliness even if they didn't.

She could keep to herself.

Matthew never appeared to worry about her uncleanliness, and when he spoke to her of Jesus, she was not shocked to hear that he had recently been chosen to follow him. She knew of Jesus, had heard of his ministry, his walks through the streets of Capernaum.

Occasionally, in the evenings, she'd venture out, but few were walking the streets then, and she never saw him. But she thought of Jesus frequently, and when Matthew's words, "I will be following him," came to her on that last visit, she cried.

"What shall I do without you?" she asked.

He touched her cheek, the wetness of her tears slipping down his forefinger.

"I will continue to pray for you," he said.

"But what about my home? How can I —"

"I have already thought of that," he said. "I am leaving my home to your family. Now, they can be nearer to you. They can help you with your needs."

"But they are getting older, surely, it will be hard for them."

"Your baby brother is no longer a baby." He smiled.

"He must be fourteen or so?"

"Almost."

Now it was her turn to smile. "I haven't seen them for such a long time."

"I know."

When Matthew grew silent a sliver of fear raced through her soul. "What?" she asked.

"There's something else."

The foreboding tone in which he spoke reminded her of something that had happened long ago when she was small. She had gone out with her mother shopping, and they had stopped only a moment. "I am tired," her mother had said. "Let's rest awhile." And the two of them had sat away from the others eating the grapes they had just purchased.

"I want you to remember how much I love you," her mother said. "There will come a time when you will truly know this, but for now, I want you to have faith in what I'm going to tell you. There will come a day when you will have true faith in the Messiah. He will come as he has promised."

Jesus had come. Was he the Messiah? She had never seen him, but she believed in her mother's words just as she did now.

The pain had been almost unbearable today; if anything, the pain was increasing in its intensity as she grew older.

Matthew was a patient man. He'd stopped talking as she reflected on her life and only began speaking when she regained eye contact with him.

"Your mother is gone," he said.

"When?"

"Early this morning. The mourning was difficult, but she is buried."

A sob escaped her lips. "Why —"

She'd almost asked, "Why didn't you tell me so that I could go?" but she knew the answer. She could not go out.

"How did it happen?"

"Like you, she has been sick for a long time."

"She was always tired."

"She could do no more."

"How is Father?"

"Well enough."

"He will not make it without Mother."

"He is stronger than you think."

"A drink?" she asked.

He stood. "No. I must be going. I have overstayed my welcome."

"Please."

He sat, and reaching his hand to find hers he squeezed it. "You are a brave woman. What can I do?"

"Get a message to Father for me. Tell him that I am all right. Tell him how much I love him."

"I will."

"And Matthew? Do not mourn for me. I have been happy here. Really. The words of God you have brought me through the years have connected me to what is truly important. The letters from my family have kept me going. My body might be unclean but my heart is pure."

Touching her hand one last time he left her. "I will miss you," he said. "But do not worry, you are not forgotten — nor forsaken."

Once the light was extinguished, she cried lonely and heart-filled tears for her mother. As her heart finally drifted back to Matthew, another revelation came to her, one that would never have been in place had she not lived here. It would not be easy to go on without Matthew, but she would.

The next morning, as the pain engulfed her once again, she cried for her mother and the only friend she'd ever had. God was there, but two loving, living persons were gone. She comforted herself in the knowledge that she'd see her brother, and that her father would be close by to help her soon, yet there was an ache inside her heart that couldn't be filled.

Bringing out the words of God she read:

"...I will come *into* thy house in the multitude of thy mercy: *and* in thy fear will I worship toward thy holy temple".

Anna had never been allowed inside the Court of the Women, though she was worthy in every other respect. His spirit had been here, hadn't it? Being ritually unclean she could not pass beyond the fence surrounding the outer courts. Before the plague, she'd sat within the Women's Hall and looked on the temple's strong walls, had watched the people coming and going, happier when they were going. She'd searched her soul for the time that she might step within the inner walls.

But the time had never come.

Still, hope was strong as she walked to the door and reached for the water jug. Bringing it inside she placed it on the table, reached for a cup, and took a drink. The water was still cold as if he'd just left it.

Tears sprang to her eyes, but it was no use dwelling on what she couldn't have. She must remain grateful for her blessings.

Reaching again for the words she read:

"Have mercy upon me, O LORD; for I *am* weak: O LORD, heal me; for my bones are vexed. My soul is also sore vexed:

but thou, O LORD, how long? Return, O LORD, deliver my soul: oh save me for thy mercies' sake".

"Heal me..." The words spoke to her soul.

Could she be healed?

Matthew would be leaving soon if he wasn't gone already. Jesus. She just had to see him before it was too late. But, how could she go?

She reached for the unassuming shawl, one left by Matthew one morning. She would keep her head bowed, her face covered, until the last minute. Surely, she could make it through the crowds without anyone noticing her. After such a long time. She knew the street Jesus would be traveling. It was the same street, always. She had viewed it for the last time long ago. Her street.

She would go home.

She spread the shawl over her dark hair, making sure it covered everything but her eyes. A stab of pain reached her middle, she touched it briefly, allowing the shawl to expose more of her face. No, she couldn't do that. No matter what pain she felt, she must hide her face.

Opening the door, she peeked out. Many strolled the street on which she lived, and walking further up the dirt path she saw the empty place that Matthew had once stood to collect taxes, taxes that came from travelers and traders of merchandise coming from both directions; dues for the fish caught in the sea. Who they would get to replace him she had no idea, but the thought of him – gone – sent a hollow ache within her soul.

Getting to the narrow street where Jesus walked with his disciples would not take long. But her heart thundered. The words she had read this very morning gave her the courage to place the stiff, little-used sandals on her feet.

"Let the words of my mouth, and the meditation of my heart, be acceptable in thy sight, O LORD, my strength and my redeemer".

Wouldn't she have to speak to him to get him to stop and talk with her? She would have to ask the question, wouldn't she? "Please, can you heal me? I have been suffering for many years. I have faith in thee." But, could she do it?

She shut the door behind her and looked up the street. She hadn't been a part of daylight in years, going out for cleaning during the nighttime hours when everything was in shadow. It would be alright; she could feel it. No one appeared to be staring. They didn't know her. And she was no longer a girl, but a woman. She had kept her secret well.

Still, the shawl was held tightly against her face as she walked nearer the place where Jesus was known to walk.

She thought again of the verse in Psalms that she had memorized. Could a heart speak, and if so, how would it speak? Could it say the same words as a voice could?

Yes, perhaps she need not speak.

She would touch the hem of his garment. In the touch, she would be healed. She would be whole. The blue of the tassels would be the closest thing to touching heaven that she knew. There had been others who had done the same, could not she?

That she didn't speak would not matter. She'd heard talk of the healings through the blue knotted fringes of the prayer shawl of a priest's clothing. She knew the power of remembrance because she had lived in remembrance of her family all these years. Living alone, she'd continued forward in her life by observing the commandments. The power of the priesthood was real.

These last twelve years she'd had plenty of time to pray and read. And she felt a closeness with the God of the heavens, and the God who now walked the earth.

He had to be on the narrow street at Capernaum's center with his disciples. Matthew would be there, too, her dear friend, Matthew. Just the thought of him gave her courage. Still, she kept her eyes on the ground as she journeyed past the olive presses and grain grinders, soldiers, and sellers of goods.

The words that Matthew had copied down for her filled her soul. She would yet connect with the temple no matter that she was poor. And she would be clean, and enter its sanctifying walls for the first time to worship the God who had healed her.

Reaching the narrow street, she saw her home. It was just as she remembered it. The second-story summer room had been her favorite. She remembered the guests that sometimes sheltered there; even Matthew on occasion. The smell of the grass wafted to her nose, but she wasn't sure if it was a reality or her hopeful imaginings. She remembered the various fruits her mother had dried there; how she'd carried them down for the meal at her request. She remembered her personal prayers, soft-spoken, and then unaware of the God who was yet to protect her.

Turning past her home she walked the path, taking in the sights and smells that had never really left her. Not all of the smells were good, but remembered, they became good; a part of her. The street was equally busy, and the sounds of sheep bleating met her ears as it once had.

Someone pushed against her roughly, but she continued, holding her white shawl even closer to her face. Peering in front of her she noticed a large group approaching; mostly men, but that was not unusual. And then she saw him. There was no mistaking Jesus, though she'd never seen him before.

Where could she go?

Searching the body of walkers, and finding available space, she pushed her way through them. He was almost to her, and then she couldn't see him. "Please, God," she prayed.

Drawing close to the ground, her stomach and back drew pain, but she would not think of it. Not now. There, he was right there, passing her. "If I may but touch his garment, I shall be whole." All she had to do was reach out and… touch.

There was a sudden stop.

Anna breathed in. Something had changed.

There was no more pain. The blood… the plague, she could feel it no more.

As her mind and heart thought on these things, a voice she didn't recognize, though she knew it, spoke: "Who touched my clothes?"

And then Matthew's voice: "Thou seest the multitude thronging thee, and sayest thou, Who touched me?"

Anna trembled. What could she do? Say?

She bowed her head, and falling before Him confessed, "Jesus, it was I."

It was the blue in his eyes she saw first. Penetrating. Loving and wise. He knelt before her, and taking her face in his gentle hands, said: "Daughter, thy faith hath made thee whole: go in peace, and be whole of thy plague."

Just as she'd spoken to Him only moments before with her heart and with her lips, He'd spoken to her silently and with His words. She no longer heard the commotion around her. The bleating of sheep, the voices of those coming and going into the city of Capernaum. Only Him.

The warmth of his presence filled her with love overflowing. He knew her.

And she knew He was the Messiah.

Christ sits at the bedside of Jairus's sickening daughter - Etching by E.F. Mohn after G.C. von Max, 1840-1915

Jairus's Daughter
Matthew 9

Adina was delicate from birth. She didn't take her first breath easily, and her last breath was hard and quick. Before that terrible day, Adina spent much of her time running when she had been commanded by the physician, not to. She would run early in the morning when peering eyes were closed and Capernaum was settled.

She would run, and then she would sneak back into the house, change her clothes, and get back into bed before rising again – this time with the whole family.

She had two siblings. A brother named Tomer, he was the eldest, and a brother named Yaron, whom, her parents said, must have been yelling before he was born. He came out red. Tomer, on the other hand, was as calm as the wind blowing through the palm trees out front. It took a lot for him to scream.

Adina was smaller than most babies, and Mother and Father were always trying to fatten her up. Instead, while she remained willowy and thin, her brothers grew as thick as sycamore trees.

She was always commanded to walk slow, stay in bed as long as possible, and not strain herself. When her father fished, and her brothers helped, she was expected to lie down and rest.

Running was the only thing that freed her. She would dress, put her best sandals on, the ones with the thick straps, peek out the door, and when she saw no one, escape.

She ran once every morning for over a year before she was caught.

A man, her neighbor, had found her in the fields. He was socially respected, as was her father Jairus, a synagogue official. He lived in a fine house, too, and was angry seeing her in the darkness. He, himself, had not been able to sleep. The air was thick with heat that night, and he'd withdrawn from his house only to see something moving in the distance. The full moon had uncovered the soul, and he was determined to find out who it was.

He did not expect her.

"What are you doing?" he'd asked, placing his large hand on her slim shoulders, the light of his lamp shining into her eyes.

"Nothing," she stuttered.

"It looks like something to me. You should be in bed."

"This is the only time I can run."

"I did not think you could run," he'd answered.

"But I can run. It is the only thing I can do. Please, don't tell Father."

"You are a sick girl."

"I am not sick. I am only small," she'd said.

He'd looked into her eyes then, big round eyes with dark pupils. The moon's rays cascaded down his back and lit up his face.

"You are sick. And I am taking you home."

He'd taken her hand then, roughly. She'd pulled from him.

"You must come – now!" he urged.

She had gone with him.

At the door, he'd knocked. She was 10 and could have done it herself. No one came. He let go of her hand. "Go, get your parents. I will wait here."

It was a strange request, so early in the morning, but she had obeyed. In only moments her parents would know that she had disobeyed. She would be locked inside the house forevermore.

She woke her mother first. Mother was sensible and would not yell. She opened her eyes slowly and reached for Adina's hand. "What is it? Are you sick?" she asked.

"No. Our neighbor is at the door. He wants to speak with you."

She nudged Father. "Husband!" she whispered, though the whisper was louder than a whisper usually was. Her father turned from his side and looked up. "Get to bed!" he said.

"Someone is at the door," Mother said.

Father sat up. "Now? Are you sure?"

Mother looked in her direction, then turned briefly away from her and lit the lamp. It sparkled and glistened. Father rubbed at his eyes. "What could Noah want at this hour?" He looked at her.

"He's at the door, Father."

Father got up, put on his robe, and retreated to the door. Opening it, he blinked into the eyes of his friend, who had his lamp lit in front of him.

"I found your daughter outside." He pointed beyond the house. "She was in the fields."

Father turned. His eyes burned her skin. "What were you doing – out?" he asked.

"I needed some time alone," she said, which was a half-truth she hoped her neighbor wouldn't correct.

"She was running."

Noah was a good man. He went to synagogue with Father, was asked to perform temple duties, and took his family to hear Jesus' words on occasion, though the latter duty had dwindled in recent weeks.

"Thank you," he told the neighbor, and in seconds the door was shut and he was staring down at her.

"What have Mother and I told you about running?" he asked.

"I am not to do it," was her reply.

"Then why? And why at such an ungodly hour as this?"

She'd shrugged then. A poor answer, she knew that now, now that she was almost twelve and had learned some things about adults. Firm answers always got a second look. Indecisive ones, only caused further problems.

Mother wiped her eyes before she spoke. "You might have been hurt, or taken," she said.

"This is a safe place. Even you have said so, Mother."

"Still." She'd reached for her then, taking her daughter into her arms. "Still…"

"I will not have it," said her father. "Return to bed. We will talk more about this at first light."

She'd nodded, extricating herself from her mother and returning to her bed. But she hadn't slept. As she watched the walls, dark like soot, she counted the imaginary sheep that were there. She recounted the many times she stayed home while the others went out. She went on short walks. Only short walks. She went to get food with her mother, but only when they needed little. She walked with her father to fish at the northern shore, but the visits were short. Her brothers would go often and for much longer periods.

But her infirmity, as the others called it, had kept her within short distances to home for as long as she could remember. It wasn't fair. Just because she was smaller than the others?

Sure, sometimes she felt weak. She had to sit, especially after running, but running free had never been an issue for her only for a few minutes. Her heart, yes, it had beat wildly, like it was going to jump from her skin, but it never had, and before too long it had calmed and was beating normally again. Only a few times had she gotten dizzy, and only once had her chest hurt. She'd stopped, sat, and tried to breathe evenly. When the pain had stopped, she'd returned to her bed.

But now, now things were different. Almost two years later, her parents had gained the help of her brothers. There was no escaping at night.

Adina managed to run in her dreams. She ran in her mind at the supper table. She ran as she fished, as she walked the short distance to the market with her mother. Inside, where no one could see, she ran, and the feeling was glorious.

Still, there were times Adina really wanted to run. And she imagined that one early morning, she would somehow be able to escape, though her brothers took turns sleeping by the front door. Though her sandals were placed in her Mother and Father's room at night. She would sneak out without them. The windows were nearer the roof; she couldn't even reach them standing on her bed, but she would have to get outside – somehow.

Once, only once mind you, she had made it beyond the front door when a hand reached out. "Got you!" Yaron said.

She tried and failed to escape. He had her by the wrist, and suddenly one wrist became two.

"Just for a minute… please?"

"Father would have my hide," he said.

"You don't have to tell him."

"Always the secretive one, are you? What would you do for me if I let you go?"

"I...I would do all your chores."

"You mean you'd take care of the animals?"

She nodded. They had many animals: goats and sheep and donkeys, even chickens, though she'd always taken care of the last part.

"What about the rest?"

"What rest?"

"The fishing. All the long walking with Father?"

"I would enjoy that," she said. "When can I start?"

"Never!"

"But you said..."

"I was just teasing you. Go to bed."

"I will not."

"Go to bed or I'll tell on you. I'll say you escaped from me and went running into the fields."

"You wouldn't! You wouldn't tell them that. You'd get in trouble for letting me escape!"

Yaron rubbed his chin. He already had prickly hairs growing out of it.

"Go to bed!"

"I will not!"

The yelling had awoken another besides Yaron. In an instant, Tomer was standing there. "What's going on?" he asked, rubbing his eyes.

"Our sister, here, is trying to escape."

"Why?"

"To run of course."

"I wasn't going to run. Just…walk a little."

"She was going to run."

Adina turned from them and skipped to her room. The skipping hadn't affected her at all. Her heart was fine, and her brothers were worried for no reason. She would escape if it was the last thing she did.

A few weeks went by before the opportunity presented itself. The air was like a hot rag over her eyes, and it was hard to breathe. Her brothers and father were taking a well-needed trip away from her, and she and her mother would get some alone time where talk changed from fishing and business to cooking and grooming.

As a young woman, she was expected to take care of herself, even if she never found a husband, which was doubtful. Adina wondered if she'd be able to marry. Surely, she would not be able to have children. The birthing process was difficult, even for healthy girls, and she had been told many times by her mother – not through spoken words but through looks – that bearing children was not expected. It was enough responsibility to take care of her own needs.

The early morning hours settled in before Adina left the house. She didn't retrieve her sandals but tiptoed barefoot to the door. Stopping briefly, she listened for footsteps that never came. Pulling the door open and pushing it closed, she retreated into the hot air. At first, she did not run, but walked, hoping if she was careful, no one, especially not the neighbor, would see her.

Success.

She was in the field, and the narrow streets in front of her house and others nearby were empty. Into the field, she plunged. It was only in running that she truly felt the hand of God. It was like he was there, running beside her, helping her forward, giving her the strength to pump her legs and reach for the stars. The grass was long, thick, and dry. It whipped at her legs as she danced and twirled and ran.

The stars were truly singing. She could almost hear them as she leaped and trounced through the fields behind her home. Oh, the joy! The heat of the day whisked past her cheeks, her hair, open and free flew behind her, like a great wind! She spun, opening her arms to catch the hug from the heavens she was sure would be hers, when a sudden pull stopped her.

Her heart was thundering. She must sit. Moments later, the earth was still spinning and she could not breathe! Trying to calm her thundering heart, she placed her palm over it the way she had always done and thought of God and his healing power. Now it would calm. She would be alright.

But she wasn't all right, and at the last gasp of air, she thought she could feel him, his loving arms around her.

"I see you've been running," he said.

She could not see his face.

"I am only free when I run."

"I am taking you home."

"To Mother and Father?"

"Is that where you want to go?"

"Yes."

"That is well. You have much to do yet."

She wondered what he meant. She took care of the chickens. Helped her mother cook. Walked short distances with her family. Went to the market.

"Will you heal me?" she asked.

"Is that what you want?" he asked.

"Yes. I want to return to my family."

"Even now, your mother, who found you in the field, is running to find your father. In time, your father will find my son."

"Jesus?"

"Yes. See, he and the twelve are stepping out of the boat. He is begging my son to come to his home because of you."

"Am I dead?"

"No. You are sleeping."

"Why have they stopped? Why the crowd of people?

"Behold, Anna. She has an issue of blood. For twelve years this sickness has been upon her."

Adina watched as a woman spoke to Jesus. She watched as she touched his clothes. Jesus looked down. She heard the words he spoke to her. She could see that the disease had left her body, that she was made whole.

Through the crowd that had gathered around the woman, she saw her father and the disciples of Jesus. A man approached. He looked like a ruler from the synagogue.

"Thy daughter is dead: why troublest thou the Master any further?"

Was her father troubling the Master?

"Be not afraid, believe, and she will be made whole," Jesus said to the ruler of the synagogue. Then standing, he asked Peter, James, and John the brother of James to follow him. Her father looked afraid. Tears were in his eyes. Adina had never seen him this way.

She watched as her father ran down all of the streets she knew. And when they reached her house, all the people who had followed – and there were many – were commanded to stay without the door.

Her brothers stood within the door, and Peter, James, and John and her father went inside. All others were commanded to withdraw. She was lying still, covered with the white blanket her mother had sewn for her.

And he was there. Jesus.

"Give place: for the maid is not dead, but sleepeth."

Everyone laughed. The minstrels outside. Some of the neighbors. But not her brothers at the door. Not her mother, her father. Tears glistened on their cheeks.

"Is it time?" she asked.

"It is," the Father answered.

In the next breath, she was there. Her heart felt better somehow. And she could feel Jesus' hands on her head. She could feel the heat of the day, the warmth of the blanket that had been removed from her face. She could feel Him. She could feel *this*.

"Damsel, I say unto thee, arise." He took her by the hand.

She opened her eyes.

Her mother was astonished. It was as if the tears had stopped mid-stream. Her father stared down at her. Her brothers, both of them, raced to her side. They said nothing but their eyes said everything. They were amazed!

"She is hungry," Jesus said. "Give her something to eat."

She was hungry, yes. And she would eat, and hug her parents and kiss her brothers, and they might even let her. And then she would run. Run.

Raising the Young Man of Nain – Paolo Veronese, 1560s

Naamah's Son
Luke 7

Naamah lived a quiet life. Her time was spent tending to her house and caring for her son, Ahinoam (Ahi). Although she'd heard of Jesus of Nazareth, and the miracles he performed, she'd never seen him. Still, at times like today, she felt the sweet whisperings of something within her heart that she couldn't quite place.

Ahi, who was fifteen at the time his father died, had learned how to care for the family's wheat in the small farming village near Mount Moreh. With the training of his father at an even earlier age, Ahi had learned the skills of sowing, hoeing, and grain harvesting; labor that began after the first winter rains had subsided and concluded with the harvest that began in June. The wheat harvested and then sold provided a living for Naamah and her son – but just enough.

Still, Nain was a beautiful and pleasant place. Just east of the Jezreel Valley, the town sloped to a single path, where occasionally someone came to visit, though rarely to Naamah and her son. And yet, there was privacy enough, and plenty of room to live out one's days.

There were neighbors, of course, but not many; and the homes or places of refuge needed extra care as they were built of mudbrick, their flat roofs anchored with beams, covered with pine planks, and topped with clay. The floor was dirt, but Naamah swept it daily, knowing that God looked upon all of his children in kindness, whether they were wealthy or not.

Thrice, her husband had repaired the walls to their one-room shelter after the shaking of the earth which came randomly and without warning, but weekly the walls still needed mending. Adjoining the house, they had a space prepared for a donkey and two goats. Stairs from the outside led to the roof where they slept, (where food was stored in wooden containers for the winter, and dried fruits and vegetables were kept), and paid their devotions to God.

Since the death of her husband; her only son spent his time daily in the fields, and although she joined him at times, it was her son who fed and clothed them. And it was he who harvested and measured the wheat for sale.

Cut by a scythe blade made from thin pieces of rock set in a curved handle made of wood, the wheat planted at the end of October was currently being gathered to be carted off and sold. It was June already. Ahi was busy with the chore the entire month. She would repair the walls. Cook the meals. Tend to the animals. Weave for her and her son. And she would see him briefly in the morning, and then again at night.

He was tired today as she laid out his straw mat for sleeping.

"Thank you, Mother," he said, yawning, stretching his long arms above his head just as he'd done as a child. "How was your day?"

"Same as always." She sat on her mat and looked over at him. His dark hair spread to the left and right of his face like fingers. Now that he was twenty, he was no longer a child but a man. He might have left her for a young bride, but the boy, turned man, was still here.

The skies were darkening, and the little light they had from the stars would not hold them much longer.

"I am worried about you," she said.

"Me?" he moaned, and she could see his eyes closing.

"You work too hard."

"You mean like a farmer?"

She laughed. It was his joke.

"You are looking tired."

"I am tired," was his reply.

"After the harvest, I want you to take it easy for a while. Perhaps we can spend some time with Jesus of Nazareth."

Ahi sat up. "He is busy. His teaching takes him everywhere but here." He stood slowly, and padding to his mother, he sat on her mat and looked up at the sky. "It's almost like angels are up there," he said.

"They *are* up there," she countered.

He laughed. "You know what I mean."

"I know you need some sleep."

"I'll sleep in a minute. Let's talk about our trip."

"You mean it?"

"Of course. After the harvest is over, we'll go. It will be hot, we'll need plenty of water, but we can take the donkey. You can ride."

"You'll walk?"

"We'll take turns if that makes you feel better."

She smiled. "It will be a wonderful visit. I have heard beautiful things about Jesus. There have been friends, neighbors who have seen him. I want to see him."

"And we will, Mother. But right now, I think I need some sleep."

Her son arose, and in doing so, reached out and touched his mother on the cheek. "I love you," he said.

"I love you," she answered, laying down and looking up at the stars just before prayer. What a comfort her husband had been. How loving. How hard he'd worked. Just like his son. Just like Jesus of Nazareth would be.

The next morning, she arose, rolled up her sleeping mat, and prayed to God. The grass played easily on her legs as she kneeled and searched her heart:

"Hear, O God, bless my son. Give him the strength to do his work. Give me the strength to do all that thou hast asked of me. In my loneliness, comfort my heart. I love thee with all my heart, soul, and might. Thy words shall be upon my heart. I shall teach them diligently to my son. I shall talk of them when I sit in my house, and when we walk by the way. When I lie down and when I rise. Blessed art thou, O Lord, God of Abraham, God of Isaac and God of Jacob, Most High God, Lord of heaven and earth, my shield and the shield of my fathers. Blessed art thou, O Lord, the shield of Abraham. In thanksgiving, I thank thee for my life, though difficult the way. I feel of thy joy in the presence of thy Son. Amen".

Upon arising, Naamah rolled up her bedroll and stored it inside the shelving her husband had made for her. Her son was already up, his bedroll placed neatly nearby. She wondered if he'd eaten.

Returning to the cooking area, a circle of stones with a fire at its center, she smiled.

Yes, he'd eaten, and smothered the burning fire as was his custom when he arose earlier than she. The room was still fairly warm and she could see Ahi had already prepared the morning meal from the dough she'd set aside the night before.

She reached for the freshly made bread he had left her, and grabbed a handful of figs, placing them in a narrow dish. She needed to milk the goats first because she had slept longer than planned.

Their braying filled her ears as she entered the stall just off the side door of their home. She would tend to the straw too and sweep the room where they lodged. The smell was horrible, unbreathable, but Naamah was used to it, as she was used to most things now.

Her worry had amplified, though her husband had taken on part of the worry while he was here. Chores were drawn out – more was expected of her. Her son, though thoughtful, often forgot to help her with the things her husband naturally gravitated to, whether out of interest or love for her.

Still, her life was good. She prayed. She worked. She thought of her son and the day she would pass and he would marry. She knew he wouldn't marry while she yet lived, though he and his wife might have taken her into their household as some of their neighbors had done. But there was too much work, her son said. Too much to do, to spend time searching for a wife. Besides, in this small village, all of the choices had already been looked over and found wanting.

Her hand reached out to the donkey. The bucket of milk was already at the door's entrance waiting for her. Patting him lightly on the back she said, "It won't be long now. Like, Mary, I will ride you, and we will go and see this teacher for ourselves."

The donkey brayed as if knowing her words, and she left him. She wiped her hands on her dress and folded her fingers around the handle of the milk bucket.

She ate alone, but the whisperings continued. It was as if he sat by her now, telling her truths she had learned as a child. Truths of hope, of salvation, of giving. Before Jesus was born, prophets had foretold of his birth. Isaiah had prophesied, "For unto us a child is born, unto us a son is given: and the government shall be upon his shoulder: and his name shall be called Wonderful, Counsellor, The Mighty God, The Everlasting Father, The Prince of Peace". A virgin would be the Messiah's mother, and the baby's name would be Immanuel.

Sometimes, unlike today, she felt her husband nearby. She could almost smell his clothes as he came in for breakfast, the scent of the animals on him. But today, something was different. The smells were there, traveling through the fabric of her clothes, but it was as if something like spring entered her nostrils and filled her soul.

What could it be?

When the voice called to her she was still in her reverie, thinking of them. The teacher she would soon meet and the husband she would see in time.

"Yes?"

It was her neighbor, Judith. She, like many women who lived in the small village, had little time for visiting, but when one arrived at your door, it was like spring had arrived no matter the season. Perhaps this is what she'd felt before turning and seeing her there.

"You must come – at once!"

"Why? What has happened?"

"Your son!"

Naamah turned from her food and touched the hand of her friend. Judith pulled her through the doorway. It was a warm morning, like every other morning. As the warmth brushed against Naamah's cheeks she thought of her son. Something had happened to her son, something so horrible her friend had not been able to speak it.

Her skin trembled as if she was cold, and as her mind searched her heart, she remembered his words to her from the night before, "I love you, Mother."

Near the threshing floor, just outside of the village, her friend stopped. "We did all we could," she said, pointing to an area where the neighbors were gathered. "Please, know that I am here for you."

Time slowed as Naamah ran, though this time she wasn't guided by the strong arm of her friend. She fell. Bruised, she stood and continued to run until the dots in the distance had grown large and the tall forms moved as she brushed by.

It was her son, and he was bleeding.

She fell to her knees. "Oh, God! Save my son!" she cried, but no breath escaped his tongue. His chest, dirty from the work of harvesting was wet. "My son!"

A hand reached for her. She shrugged it off.

"Ahinoam, my son... Please."

Her strength gone, Naamah collapsed. She could smell the sweat of his body. The stillness, the silence of his chest. "Oh, son!" she sobbed.

Again, a hand reached out.

"Leave me alone!" she screamed, feeling nothing, for suddenly her heart was stone.

Moments later, she learned the horrifying truth. Her son, weak and dizzy, had been warned to rest. Instead, he'd kept working and had fallen on his scythe blade, ending his own life.

When the wheat arrived an hour later, wheat that her son should have brought in to her from the harvest, she cried again, and would not eat. Judith, who was at the threshing floor when the accident occurred, could not console her friend, and after four long hours of trying, returned to her own house.

Naamah was alone.

Not even God could console her now.

Nain was no longer beautiful. It was no longer sweet.

Perhaps, thought Naamah, I will die.

But Naamah did not die.

Her son's eyes were closed by someone who had witnessed his death. She kissed him and washed the sweat and dirt from his body. Anointing him with spikenard – a gift left to her, she knew not by whom, Naamah remembered their last night together as mother and son, taking in the stars, smelling the green grass. She remembered the prayer uttered just this morning.

It was late, morning for the burial would have to be soon enough.

There was no time to think about life without him, but she did. There was no time to wonder how she would be able to live to eat to sustain herself without her son, but she wondered. She did not sleep, and as the next day arrived, she was ready.

It was early, but the morning was already warm, and the burial could not be delayed. Friends had come to say their farewells all through the night, and she had chosen those whom custom warranted should carry the bier to the grave. None were family, but dear ones which she had grown up with; others she had met through her husband, yet some knew of her, what she had already lost, and what little she had now to sustain her.

She was grateful for the compassion, especially now.

The day was overcast. Once outside the door, the procession began, and the tears and the wailing of the women leading the group created a striking contrast to what would have been a usual morning for most of these women tending to their children.

Naamah had chosen to bury her son beside her husband in a shaft near the wheat fields where they had both worked. Within the area was a sacred tree. She had spent many hours of her youth playing in its shade, and it was the place where she had been married to her husband – though a canopy had been provided as well – double the shade for a couple who would spend years together loving each other. She thought of him now, felt his presence as she followed the bier to its final resting place.

Her son would want her to be strong, she knew that. She could feel his love drifting through the warm morning air, could feel his touch, and the joy that had sparkled in his eyes when he told her of their time away to visit the Master.

It would be soon, he'd said. Right after the harvest.

As the women wailed in front of her Naamah bowed her head. She loved her son but now he was gone, and she had no one left. He was with her husband, and the two, surely, watched her even now as the tears fell. They would be with her in spirit, Naamah knew that. But how might she live alone? Many had told her that when her husband died it was a sign of God's judgment upon her. And now, with her son gone, was God punishing her again?

She thought of the hungry, the starving, without even a coin for food. Now she was 'the hungry'. The warm wind had picked up since she'd left her shelter, but she held on, thinking of her son. Oh, how she loved him!

It was in the gasp that Naamah thought to look up. It was as if the smell of spring was somehow here at last, and that, after all, she would not be burying her son.

It was his eyes she saw first. Blue, the color of the sky when not weeping. They were clear and penetrating and filled with love.

It was He.

But how could He have known?

Even from Capernaum, it took at least ten hours to reach her village. To come so soon He had to have arisen early and walked the entire night. He had to have known her plight without anyone telling Him.

She was near the gate of the city, an entrance used by every traveler. It wasn't a fancy entrance. A simple wooden arch filled the sky above and offered respite.

"Weep not," He said and touched the bier.

The procession stopped. It was not customary to touch the bier – it being unclean, but Jesus had.

Naamah waited. She thought of her son, the boy turned man, now dead. She drew in a breath watching Him – Jesus of Nazareth, the one her son had said he was going to take her to see. And now he was here. The sweet whisperings of truth met her ears.

"Young man, I say unto thee, Arise."

Ahinoam's face, grey and cold only moments before – colored – she could see the blood returning and his skin warming. As she watched, gazing at the miraculous scene, he sat up.

"Mother," he said.

There was an audible gasp from the crowd of friends she had grown to love as Jesus reached for him. Taking her son by the hand, he helped him to his feet and brought him to her.

In moments, amidst the praise and glory of her friends – some who sang, "A great prophet is risen up among us. God hath visited his people," Ahi embraced her. The hug was warm, and just as she remembered it.

Jesus Anointing – Alexander Bida, 1874

Rachel's Jar

Luke 7

Rachel believed in the power of faith for everyone except herself. Though her friends had married well, she had not. She was poor and she and her husband had no children.

She'd read the stories from the scriptures about Mother Eve, the courageous one, who, along with her husband, Adam, created the beginning of all human life, of Esther, the great prophetess who delivered her people from death. Of one, Sarah, who bore a child in her old age, and virtuous Rebekah, who sat at the well, awaiting the arrival of her husband, Isaac, though she knew it not. Even her namesake, Rachel, who had to wait fourteen years to wed Jacob, and could not have children, in the end, was blessed with a great posterity – greater than even she could have realized.

When her own husband left her for another, she was left to ponder over her life and the little she had. It didn't seem fair that she must live alone, and make a meager living serving others blessed with more abundance.

The arrival of Jesus to the city of Jerusalem created interest, and the more often he came and went, the more eager Rachel was to hear him. But the days were long and labor-intensive. Either she was working to sell vegetables or cleaning to have a place to eat and sleep.

She hadn't recently offered herself as "payment" as some in the village would speak of, but kept to herself, and found jobs here and there as they became available.

Perhaps, yes, she could be grateful for that.

Though she knew of Jesus she'd never really met him. She'd seen him only once at a distance in the street. Her heart had burned then, like a tiny flame reaching for kindling to increase its warmth. She wondered at the sight of him, his slow strides, how the people flocked to be near him, like sheep. But she had not approached – could not approach.

It was not easy for her to study the word of God. She did it secretly and found that the study helped to ease her fears of death when it would finally come and no one would mourn for her. She had learned to read Hebrew as a child from a father who had lived the Jewish law and had not been afraid to profess it or even share it with her. But he had died long ago, and after that, almost a year later to the day, so had her mother. She was their only child.

Marriage had come early to her, and she had been happy for the proposal soon after her fourteenth birthday. But the marriage had never been good.

Without a husband to provide, hunger quickly found its place within her soul – she knew she must make a living for herself. At the onset, she had done what she could to keep herself fed, sleeping with whoever wanted her, stealing what she could, spending her nights in the open air. But later, as she grew to maturity, she was able to do honest work in homes where shelter was provided for her.

And while men's eyes wandered, hearing of her past, she would tell them that she had changed and they would mock her. She had been forced more than once, and the abuse that threatened to take away her soul had not. She would not let it.

She wasn't sure when the idea came to her that she might provide something for herself besides the clothing that adorned her body, or the money that kept her fed and sheltered, but perhaps the scriptures had breathed life into her. No matter how bad it got, she'd always tried to find her way back to God. And He had always taken her in.

No one could understand this. But He could.

She'd spotted the small, alabaster jar of spikenard on its stand at a booth where vegetables were sold. It seemed an odd place, but as she looked near it, there were flowering plants of different varieties; rather than the honeysuckle had produced such an oil. The perfume had come from China, so said the florist, and, as she remembered, it was very expensive.

"Can I smell it?" she asked.

The florist, a stout woman with two chins, frowned. "I don't think so."

"But I have the money."

The woman raised her eyebrows.

"You are getting married then."

"No." She blushed, remembering her wedding night, the sweet aroma of spikenard filtering through the room as a covenant of love. "No."

"Show me your coins."

She opened her hand revealing more than 300 denarii, two years' worth of wages.

"Fine. You can smell."

The honey was evident. The sweetness. She closed her eyes, breathing it in.

"That's enough. The money?"

73

Rachel placed the coins in the woman's hands. It was all the money she had. She had forgotten to save a portion of it for food for the coming week.

She capped the amber nard and placed the alabaster jar in her deep pocket, the one she had before used to carry her utensils for cooking in, and smiled down at the woman.

"Thank you."

"Perhaps it will keep you in the straight way," the woman said, turning from her.

But Rachel had to cook for a large family tonight, and could not be bothered by the woman or her words. Perhaps she could take a few of the scraps from the family's dinner which would be later. If not, she would open the jar and smell the sweetness. It was the only beautiful thing she owned – would ever own. It was worth it.

She hid the jar beneath her blankets most nights, and during the day, as she worked, she carried it with her, never leaving the jar out of sight. She'd never used it on herself, never rubbed the sweet oil against her skin, but she could smell the heavenly sweetness whenever she wished. Other than the scriptures it was her only joy.

As the months passed, Rachel learned more and more about Jesus and his kind ways. She also learned of how others treated him. She knew of the treatment others could lend when they didn't understand. And many didn't understand Jesus.

He was the greatest teacher she had ever known, though she had never heard his sermons from his own lips, with her own ears. It was through others, mostly in passing, that she heard of his greatness in healing others, in speaking truth, in allowing all to come unto him.

Just recently, he had brought a young man back to life in the village of Nain. Her heart had burned at the words, and she'd remained still, closing her eyes, breathing in the scent of honey as she thought about the boy's mother and her joy, as well as the joy of the boy, safely returned to his mother.

Could she come unto Him?

It was in the silence of one evening of reflection that she heard someone speaking on the roof. She was preparing for bed, near one of the sheep, when the words came down to her ears.

"That man has been invited to Simon's home, a Pharisee. He has been asked to dine, and Jesus has accepted."

"Where?"

"Up the road."

"But a Pharisee. He should know better."

"Set a better example, you mean."

"Exactly. What is a teacher doing taking in a false prophet?"

The other man laughed. "Some would say it's the other way around."

"The Pharisee, a false prophet?"

"Of course."

"But Jesus doesn't respect Jewish law. He heals on the Sabbath. Takes drunks in as if they are his best friends..."

"Maybe they are the only ones who will be his friend."

Another laugh, this time, louder.

"I just don't understand it. Have you ever heard this Jesus teach?"

"Some. He comes to the synagogue. He speaks quite eloquently for a false prophet."

"Eloquent, you say? More like someone trying to get himself killed."

"Do you think it will happen? There is talk..."

Rachel wiped at the tears that had formed on her cheeks. She reached for the sheep at her side. It bleated in thankfulness. In all the years she had slept in stalls and caves and in homes where places for animals was the rule of things, she had never thought that a poor, single woman with nothing to her name could help a teacher who spoke Truth.

Placing her hand in her pocket, the jar was still there. It was smooth against her fingers, and as she lifted it out, she knew.

Another tear fell. Placing the jar back into her pocket she stood. The skies had darkened, but she knew of the home, or would surely know of the home when she approached it. Simon the Pharisee was an outspoken man. She had watched him leave his home and return, only to leave it again the next day.

Jesus had a following, but he also had men and women who cursed him and wished for his death. While some were bold, talking about him while they walked the streets and sat on their roofs during the evenings, many more spoke about him hatefully behind their hands to friends and passersby.

She was a sinner, and yet, surely, he would let her in, just as he had done the others who needed him. But how should she approach?

She walked the dusty path with no light to guide her way other than the various windows lit up for the evening meal. The road was almost silent as she thought about the man called Jesus. Her heart burned at the thought of meeting him, but her mind was filled with pain. She had not repented as the words of God instructed; she'd only moved on from her sins trying to live a better – cleaner life. But he'd wanted her to seek forgiveness, she knew that.

At the door, she hesitated. She did not knock. If one of Simon's servants opened the door, she would be told to leave. They would quickly see her for what she appeared to be. A harlot. Reaching for the knob, she turned it slowly, pushed it open, and walked inside.

The place was like a palace. Golden statues, marble floors, flowers of red and purple... The hall was lit with candles. Down the hall, she heard voices. They were speaking to Jesus, asking him questions about his ministry. And he was answering them simply, deeply, as she had learned Jesus was wont to do. It was the first time she'd heard his voice, and yet she knew it was Him. It was as though a calming wind brushed past her face and hair. She closed her eyes, remembering the smell of honeysuckle that emanated within the alabaster box she carried in her pocket.

At the entryway to the table where the group feasted, she stopped. A servant was standing there, and he was watching her. Quickly, before she was turned out, Rachel stepped forward, and with determination reached Jesus. The food which had been prepared and was being consumed by the guests smelled delicious. There was stew. Bread. Plenty of fruit. She still hadn't eaten, but it did not matter – not now.

Kneeling before him she reached for the alabaster box in her pocket. Opening the cover, she turned her face up to him. He said nothing but his eyes, she couldn't believe his eyes! They were like... love. She realized at that moment that she was weeping. Tears dripped from her eyes and fell to his bare feet. But she had brought no cloth with her!

Taking her long hair within her hand she brushed at the tears at his feet. Oh, the joy that filled her heart even through the tears. She was a wicked woman, and yet he did not move from her. The love... she could feel it through her skin. She could feel it from her head to her feet.

Slowly, she rubbed the ointment into his feet; spikenard that was as smooth as glass. His feet were sore, she could see that, and for the first time, Rachel realized all the miles he must have walked to be with the people. The smell of honey wafted in the air and she breathed it in, just like she'd done for many nights since its purchase. She continued to work on Jesus's feet. All was silent in the room. She could hear the wind blowing outside and the bleating of sheep. The ointment softening his skin, she kissed his feet and continued to administer.

Suddenly, he spoke:

"Simon, I have somewhat to say unto thee."

"Master, say on." Simon's voice was bold. It reminded her of her father's.

"There was a certain creditor which had two debtors: the one owed five hundred pence, and the other fifty. And when they had nothing to pay, he frankly forgave them both. Tell me therefore, which of them will love him most?"

"I suppose that he, to whom he forgave most," Simon answered.

"Thou hast rightly judged."

Rachel looked up; her duty almost finished. Jesus was looking down at her. He turned to Simon. "Simon, Seest this woman? I entered into thine house, thou gavest me no water for my feet: but she hath washed my feet with tears, and wiped them with the hairs of her head. Thou gavest me no kiss: but this woman since the time I came in hath not ceased to kiss my feet. My head with oil thou didn't not anoint: but this woman hath anointed my feet with ointment. Wherefore I say unto thee, her sins, which are many, are forgiven; for she loved much: but to whom little is forgiven, the same loveth little."

There was a reaching that Rachel had never felt before inside her heart, a sort of newness that she had never before experienced. It filled her. Like the spikenard, and its smell, like honey and sweetness on a warm day, the feeling entered her soul and remained there. "Thy sins are forgiven," Jesus said.

"My… sins?" she whispered, looking once again into his blue eyes.

"Thy faith hath saved thee; go in peace."

"Peace," she whispered, and for a moment she took in everything. The faces of those at the table, silent. The servant standing quietly behind them. The face of the Master, His face of love. No, she would never forget Him, and not this. Never this. Covering the jar, and placing it inside her pocket, she stood and turned from him, the feeling of peace following her to the door, outside the gates of one Simon the Pharisee, and back to her place of rest, where the sheep bleated at her return.

She was forgiven.

The Palsied Man Let Down through the Roof – James Tissot, 1886*1896

Yedaiah's Faith

Matthew 9

When he was young, Yedaiah's parents were against the ways of the Jews. His family lived in Qumran, a day's walk to the Sea of Galilee; his father, a scroll writer, was one of only a few who wrote of the happenings within their community.

They were the holy ones who had rejected the Jerusalem temple and the priesthood of the traditional Jews. His father had married, and he, their first-born son, had been followed by four brothers, Adonias, Gilad, Jebediah, and Darius. None of them had yet taken wives of their own, including Yedaiah who was almost thirty.

Life was good in the community of holy ones, where celibate life was respected, and life was lived closer to the earth and sea. Together, as a family and as a community, they prepared for the coming of the Messiah, when only the Essenes would triumph.

It was Yedaiah's duty to remain faithful, to share what the family had in the way of food, clothing, and shelter with others in the community. It was up to him, as the oldest, to speak of good and evil; to prepare his brothers for what was to come.

What was his surprise then, when one day, near the Sea of Galilee, he watched a man speak, a man who was unlike any man he had ever heard? He wore a cream-colored robe, and his blue eyes were calm, searching. He was speaking to a group of people. Old. Young. Men. Women. Children. Yedaiah hid from their view.

The sea was calm, and the words easy to hear:

"Blessed are the poor in spirit: for theirs is the kingdom of heaven. Blessed are they that mourn: for they shall be comforted. Blessed are the meek: for they shall inherit the earth. Blessed are they which hunger and thirst after righteousness: for they shall be filled. Blessed are the merciful: for they shall obtain mercy. Blessed are the pure in heart: for they shall see God".

Who was this man?

He crept closer, sitting at the back.

The man continued:

"Blessed are the peacemakers: for they shall be called the children of God"

He loved the sound of that. Hadn't he carried peace all the days of his life? Hadn't he helped God's children? Unlike the priests and rabbis who spoke with judgment and rudeness, he had spoken in kindness. And this man, this man who sat amongst the common and unnoticeable, spoke as if the words held a power that could calm a raging sea. Yedaiah could not speak.

"Blessed are they which are persecuted for righteousness sake: for theirs is the kingdom of heaven. Blessed are ye when men shall revile you, and persecute you, and shall say all manner of evil against you falsely, for my sake. Rejoice, and be exceedingly glad: for great is your reward in heaven: for so persecuted they the prophets which were before you.

He'd been persecuted for as long as he could remember. Why else would the Essenes have had to hide away from those "worthier" to live by the Sea of Galilee? Why else would he be living with his father, mother, and brothers, and all those who believed as he did who were part of the community?

When the sermon ended, the skies were almost dark.

Had he sat so long? He walked home, a journey that would take all night and into the morning, contemplating what he had heard from the teacher. Endless words about salt, light, about the fulfilling of the law. About the righteousness he must feel and live, the righteousness that went beyond the earth and that of the scribes and Pharisees. He had been commanded to be perfect. This he had struggled with his entire life, though he knew the words to be true.

And tomorrow he would return.

Two days later, the words spoken by Jesus, surged within his breast.

He didn't share what he'd learned with his mother, father, or brothers. This was the first time he'd ever withheld anything from them. To speak the truth was expected, even commanded. But something was different about Jesus, and he wasn't sure if his family would understand. Would they respect his words? Would he be challenged by them, and removed from the community?

Only a week following Jesus' words, Yedaiah fell. He was helping build a neighbor's roof; fitting in the beams, when the board he was standing on shifted. He fell to the ground, and for a time remembered nothing. Upon awakening, he realized he could not move his arms or legs.

All was tingling at first, and then muscle cramps set in. And then Yedaiah could feel nothing. It was as if he had no limbs, though he could see them. It was as if they belonged to someone else.

Sometimes Yedaiah could not speak; the words would not come, though he could feel them at the top of his tongue. His mother moved him more often when the sores came. In the mornings, he would be on his back, and then on his side, and then sitting up by the door. She'd leave it open for him, and he would watch the few children playing and the neighbors working. He grew angry instantly, even if a comment was meant in love, and, after a time, he stopped smiling. It was too much of an effort.

His mother took care of him. She fed him and his brothers clothed him. His brothers and father worked and served the community that he could not. He was a burden to his family and wanted to die. Why hadn't he died?

Fear filled his mind where faith had once resided, and within weeks, the words spoken by Jesus had filtered to the sky like smoke. He would never marry even if he wanted to. He'd been foolish – why hadn't he watched the placement of his feet?

He was hateful, and many who had once visited him stopped coming. Even his brothers began to avoid him. But they didn't understand! He could do nothing!

On one such night, as he thought about ways to end his life, he remembered the words of Jesus. The house he'd been standing on had fallen, and so had he, never to move again, but hadn't Jesus spoken about a house that sat upon a rock? And when the floods came and the winds blew, the house fell not because it was founded upon a rock. What had Jesus meant?

As he thought upon the words, Adonias entered the room. He looked down at him.

"I thought I should come," he said, sitting next to him.

"Why?" he asked.

"You are my brother."

"You can do nothing."

"I can read to you."

"I don't want to hear it."

84

Gilad stood in the arched doorway. "What are you talking about?" he asked.

"Nothing," Yedaiah said, for it was true.

Gilad entered, followed by Jebediah who was twenty-five. Eighteen-year-old Darius followed.

"Leave me alone," he said.

"We can't," Darius replied. "Besides, I think you have something to tell us."

"I can't move, what could I possibly have to tell you?" he answered. He'd meant it as an insult, but no one got angry.

"You have been keeping secrets," Jebediah said. "God has told me."

Yedaiah blinked. "I'm thirsty," he said.

Darius turned. A moment later, a cup was at his lips. "It's water," he said.

"No wine?"

He smiled. "No, brother. Water is better."

Yedaiah doubted it but accepted the offering.

"What secret have I been keeping?" he finally asked. He'd been in this bed for six months and had done nothing in all that time.

"Jesus, you spoke to Jesus," Adonias said.

"What?"

"Jesus. You spoke to him. What did he tell you?"

"He told me nothing. He didn't speak to me."

"But you were there, he said so."

"Who said so?"

"Mother was at the market near Galilee yesterday. Jesus spoke to her. He wanted to know how you were doing after the fall."

"He knew about my fall?"

"Said he did. He seemed concerned, too, like you had talked a lot or something."

"I have never spoken to him in my life," Yedaiah said truthfully.

"But you were there, at the mount. He said you were."

"There were a lot of people there."

"You were sitting at the back."

Jesus had *seen* him? "Where's Mother?" he asked.

"She asked that I come to you."

"You mean – we."

Gilad, who liked to witness everything happening inside and outside their house, shrugged his shoulders. "I had to know. This Jesus is a Jew. Not of the strictest sort, like the priest and Rabbis, but Mother and father are worried."

"So that's it." Yedaiah rolled his eyes."Sure, I saw him, but he never spoke to me personally. He was a great teacher."

"What did he say?" Jebediah asked. He was the most spiritual of his four brothers, and Yedaiah wondered how he would take in what he would need to tell them now. Would he think him a fool?

"He held a power I have never felt before," Yedaiah began, closing his eyes, trying to remember that day that seemed like a lifetime ago. "He spoke of holiness, false prophets, and a house that would not fall because it was founded upon a rock."

"Strange words," Gilad began.

"Strange, but penetrating," Yedaiah finished. "Jesus is like no other teacher I have ever heard, not even the enlightened ones here can compare. He was like – a ray of light. My heart felt light within me. Not just the sort of light that burns, but the lightness of a feather as it drifts to the ground once dropped.

He stopped, closing his eyes once more and fishing for more details. "He taught as one having authority, and not as the scribes" (Matthew 7:29). "If – if I could have only fallen into his open arms, I wouldn't be like I am now."

Opening his eyes, the tears streamed. "If I asked, do you think Jesus would heal me?"

The words had just left his lips when he knew. But his brothers appeared shocked at his words. They said nothing.

It would take faith. He would have to believe. But this he knew. Jesus would heal him.

"Will you take me?"

"Take you where?" Adonais asked, folding his arms.

"To Jesus."

"Father will skin us alive. Besides, Mother has already been crying. She will never let us out with you."

It was as if she heard them.

Suddenly, a face peered around the doorway. "May I come in?" his mother asked.

When his brothers nodded, she walked to his bedside. "I hear you have heard Jesus speak," she said.

"Before I fell."

Mother looked down at his legs. "What will you do now?" she asked.

"What else can I do but stay here?" he answered.

"That is good. Darius, supper is almost ready. I need your help."

When she and Darius were gone, Gilad spoke to him. "I have heard of Jesus healing in Syria. There was a servant who was paralyzed like you, in terrible pain."

"I have heard the same," Jebediah said. Jeb was a friend to everyone he knew, even, at times, and to the chagrin of his father, outsiders. Jeb had been told more than once to stay within the community.

Now, today, perhaps he'd be of some help.

"I'll need all of you," he said. "You can each take a side."

Gilad smiled. "I see what you are planning, brother."

"It is a good plan, is it not? You will just have to convince Darius."

"He is already convinced of your words, why do you think Mother took him out?"

"I will need a smaller bed. Something that can be carried."

"You really want to do this?"

Yedaiah nodded. "There is something inside me, something that is telling me that this is the right thing to do."

"Even if we could get you to Jesus, you realize it's at least a 4-day walk, brother. I'm not even counting the times we'll need to eat and rest. How do you know he'll heal you, a sinner?"

"You have come upon the answer, Jebediah. It is because I have sinned that he will heal me."

"Because you are a sinner?" Darius asked, his eyes wide. He'd returned to the room.

"Yes, Darius, because I am a sinner. You have heard the other stories of healing. I think they are true."

"I have heard that Jesus eats with sinners," Jebediah said as Darius returned to the room. He walked to his brother's bed. "It's time to eat. I will bring your dinner in as usual. Mother said I could feed you tonight."

"No, tonight we will practice," Yedaiah said. "Lift me up."

That night, unlike every other night that Yedaiah had lived since the accident, the horrible accident that had left him paralyzed from the neck down, he prayed. He prayed for himself and his brothers' safety. He prayed for healing. But most of all, he prayed for faith.

It wasn't easy sneaking out the next day. First, a bed of branches was made for him. Adonias was skilled at woodwork, and Darius was adept at keeping his mother busy while the building of his bed took place. Father, had already left for work. By noon the task was finished and his mother had left for the market.

"Do we know where he is? Surely, we don't need to walk to Syria?" Adonias asked as they loaded their brother onto the makeshift bed.

"No, but I feel of his power today," said Jeb, suddenly eager to share his thoughts. "He must be in Capernaum – and that's a much shorter walk."

"I didn't think you believed in Jesus," Yedaiah said, trying to imagine the two-day walk, with starts and stops they'd have to make to get there.

"I didn't think so either, but last night I dreamed that you were healed. We were inside a house, and there were many obstructing the door. We took you to the roof."

Darius leaned over the temporary bed of his brother. "I didn't dream, brother. But I feel something good is coming. In a few days, you will be healed."

Gilad said nothing, but his eyes spoke volumes.

With one large heft, he was lifted up by his brothers and taken outside. It would not be a short trip, but no one said a word, not even a grunt of heaviness escaped their lips as they left the house.

Kathryn Elizabeth Jones

After making numerous stops to eat, sleep and refresh themselves, three days later, they entered the city of Capernaum. Many houses sat side-by-side in the city. Many, though not all were large. All had awnings of palm leaves or brush that grew over the court of the house, keeping it shaded. It was not yet evening when families gathered on the rooftops to relax.

Yedaiah had lost count of the houses of stone they'd passed before seeing a large gathering just beyond the well of a house.

"He must be in there," Jeb said.

"People gather around him like flies," Adonias offered. He was at the front of the bed, along with Jeb. Gilad and Darius took the lighter back.

"I'll go and take a look," said Darius. "Wait here."

The boy was gone briefly, and upon his return, his eyes lit up. "He's in there all right. Along with a few Pharisees and doctors, and plenty of people. We won't be able to get in that way. I was almost stepped on."

Yedaiah smiled over at his brother. "We will find another way."

"The roof." Even as Jeb said the words, Yedaiah felt a rush of happiness fill him. Yes, that was it. The dream. He watched the surrounding people. Some looked at him with pity. Others avoided him altogether. Perhaps they would have made it through the door after all. But his brothers were already to the stairs, and he was carried to the top.

He rested on his bed for a few minutes as his brothers brushed away the palm leaves and made room for him to be lowered into the room. He remembered the fall suddenly, this time praying his brothers would not drop him.

90

But the thick ropes tied to either side of the bed were strong. And in moments he was lowered into the room. It was musty inside and as full as his brother had told him. Jesus was there, and his disciples and the Pharisees and doctors he had spoken about. The last – looked on him. Another whispered as if he couldn't believe he had come.

Still, he was there and more grateful than he could express.

Jesus smiled down at him.

Yedaiah was suddenly conscious of how he must look. His brothers had dressed him, but the journey had kicked up more than a little dust. He could feel the dirt on his face, the grittiness on his lips.

"Son, be of good cheer; thy sins be forgiven thee."

"This man blasphemeth. Who can forgive sins but God only?" a voice spoke. He looked to the right. The Pharisee who had whispered behind his hand spoke louder this time. There was mumbling all around. Some of those gathered looked at the face of the person standing next to them as if searching for approval.

Yedaiah felt a hand on his shoulder. "Wherefore think ye evil in your hearts? For whether it is easier, to say, 'Thy sins be forgiven thee'; or to say, 'Arise and walk?' But that ye may know that the Son of man hath power on earth to forgive sins, Arise, take up thy bed, and go unto thine house."

Jesus lifted his hand. In the instant the touch reached him, he felt something warm and tingling enter his body and find its way to his fingertips and legs. It was like the spirit of God filled his soul. He stood on his feet. Tears dripped from his eyes.

The wise, yet kind eyes of Jesus seemed to speak to him. "You are healed," he heard him say. "Now, go and tell thy mother and father."

Yedaiah looked up. His brothers were still at the spot where he'd been lowered. Each, in turn, smiled down at him.

"I will," he said.

The Blind and Mute Man Possessed by Devils – James Tissot, 1886 - 1894

The Father's Son

Mark 9

Sethe remembered little of his younger days. From all his father had told him, he was a bright and happy boy. He loved to play, and draw in the dirt, and keep his mother busy as he never sat still for very long.

But one day, when he was two, things began to change. His mother noticed it first; her son sitting on the floor staring at nothing. And then his body would shudder and she could not make it stop. Nothing could rouse him. Not even food. And he was often tired after he awoke from the shaking.

Sethe was taken to physicians, but no one could cure him. Some thought a demon was inside his small body. Children called him names. When he was seven, a boy pushed him down. "I can't play with you anymore," he said.

By the time he was ten, people had more than one name for him. They called him Lunatic. Dumb. Unclean.

Even when he bathed, he felt unclean. Even when he tried to sit still, he would sometimes writhe. He would fall in places where he shouldn't and get dirty. He would eat and when he awoke, wonder how he got to his bed.

The strange feeling would usually start in his belly, like an ocean wave crashing to shore; but sometimes the wave would begin in his head, and his skin would prickle like he was cold, and colored lights would flash in front of his eyes. When he awoke, the tiredness would come. It was like he hadn't slept in days.

His mother loved him. Sethe knew it because she never left home but stayed near him no matter how he was feeling. No matter how afraid she got. Sethe could see the pain, the fear in his mother's eyes, and the relief that crossed her forehead whenever he came back to her.

Sometimes, when his father took him fishing, he'd get burned from the fire. When his mother took him to the waters, he would fall in. He didn't talk much, only when it was necessary. And somehow, even then, both his mother and father knew what he was feeling even if he couldn't express it. Once, at the market, his mother had left him for only a moment. When she returned people around him were screaming terrible names at him. He was crying. He was almost ten by then and embarrassed.

It wasn't easy for his father. People in Jerusalem didn't like him. He was a follower of Jesus and fished to make a living, but few would buy the fish that he caught because they knew of his son. His father walked many miles from their home to find people who did not know he had an unclean son. Sometimes he would leave alone and go to Bethlehem, where the walk was short and the fish plentiful, at other times, he would travel with the missionaries who knew Jesus and listened to the words he taught. After a fine catch, in fish as well as Christians, he would return. But this was only after many days; and by then, Mother was crying and weary because of his constant care.

Sethe's mother taught him how to garden, how to cook, and how to read. He would practice his letters and numbers in the dirt, or peer from the window of their small house and ask his mother about the sky, the people as they walked by, or his sickness. It wasn't safe to leave, Sethe knew it. But he was lonely for someone to talk to other than his mother, and when Father was gone, he prayed that someone would come to the door, if only for a moment, and speak to him.

No one did, but the dream was real, so real, that sometimes Sethe could hear his friend as he approached. He could hear the knock, and the kind words spoken as if they'd happened. "Sethe, are you there? Come out and play with me."

Once or twice he thought he heard an animal near the door, but holding true to his promise to Father, Sethe had never opened the door for them either. Because Father always took their only animal, he didn't even have the donkey to talk to, and much of the day dragged on until he would see his father again. Sethe learned to cook at the feet of his mother, and, if nothing else, had developed a gift of combining just the right spices in whatever he cooked. Though poor, the family, because of his mother's skill, ate well.

"You are deep in thought," his mother said as they cooked the evening meal. Tonight, it was lentil soup with onion, garlic, and cumin. Mother used barley for thickening and carrots for flavor. If he ate well, an apple would be given freely.

But all was not well, and as he turned to his mother, there was a pain in his stomach and a flash of colored lights. Sethe opened his eyes. Someone was knocking at the door.

The heat of the day was narrowing, and soon, darkness would again grace the outside of their shelter.

Again, the heavy knock.

"Yes?" he asked, nearing the door for an answer.

"May I come in?"

Sethe's heart beat rapidly. Should he? But no one had come to visit before. Maybe it would be alright. He turned to find his mother, but she was no longer cooking at the fire. He opened the door. Someone tall was standing outside. His feet were large and sandaled. Looking up, he could barely distinguish the man's face in the darkness.

"Just a minute." He turned, and finding the lamp, lit it. In seconds it was in his hand and he was returning to the door.

"Hello?" he called out.

"Sethe."

"Yes?"

The man had a beard like most men in Jerusalem. But his eyes were different. Blue. The man reached forth his hand. It was strong and gentle. "I am Jesus," he said.

"I've heard of you," Sethe said. "But I'm not allowed to go out. Father speaks of you." And then a thought came to Sethe, a thought that made him wonder if he should let the man in.

"How did you know my name?" he asked.

"I have known your father for a long time," he said, still standing outside in the darkness. "He has told me of you."

"You know my father? How?"

"He is a follower."

"I am also a follower," Sethe said. "I cannot go out but I follow you."

"That is good."

"And your mother?"

"She is a follower, too. She says you are the Messiah."

"And you believe her?"

"Yes. Please come in."

It was strange and wonderful, but until that moment Sethe hadn't thought to invite Jesus in. But now, now as Jesus sat on their only low-couch he smiled over at him.

"Why do you have blue eyes?" he asked.

"They are the eyes of my Father," he said. "And you? Why are your eyes brown?"

He laughed. "For the same reason, I guess. My mother's eyes are brown, too. Most people in Jerusalem have brown eyes."

Jesus smiled. "How do you like your home?" he asked.

"It is nice enough, but I sure wish I could go out."

"What would that mean to you, Sethe?"

"To play with my friends?"

Jesus nodded.

"It would be great!" Sethe said, looking into the teacher's eyes. They spoke to him then, just as mother and father were able to speak to him, though, to his parents he talked very little. But he could talk to Jesus as if the plague was no longer inside his body. It was like he was clean and straight and smart.

The man stood. "Thank you for the visit," he said.

"Don't go."

Jesus took his hand. "You will see me again soon enough," he said.

Sethe blinked. The tears that welled there without him even knowing it, spilled down his cheeks. Closing his eyes, he wiped his face.

"There you are," his mother said. "You frightened me.

The meal is done. Are you ready to eat?"

He opened his mouth to speak, but the words would not come.

"My son, you have been resting. You fell." She showed him his left leg. "See, you scratched it against the stones."

He looked down. There was a white cloth on his leg.

"I'll bring your soup to the bed. I've already eaten, but the soup is still warm."

The next morning, when his father returned from his journey, his father spoke to them about Jesus. He'd even sold some fish. He placed the coins on the table.

"It is time to go to market," Mother said. She wiped her cheeks and gathered the money in her favorite cloth. Sethe knew the blue cloth was his mother's favorite because she never used it during cooking or cleaning. Only this.

His eyes spoke volumes. Can I go?

Usually, he stayed home with Father while Mother shopped — if he was home, but today his father hugged him. "Let's go as a family," he said. "We haven't lately made such a trip together."

It was the biggest surprise, almost as great as the dream he realized had occurred before he woke up to find his mother caring for him.

But his mother shook her head.

Father looked down at his leg.

"Your mother is right. You can't go with her to market. She will go, and we'll play a game together. Does that work?"

It didn't. "No..." he managed.

Suddenly, the lights were coming back and his head hurt. And then darkness. He floated in darkness, seeing nothing for a long time. But this time, unlike other times, he knew he was in darkness, and he knew there was only one way out. He felt the presence of the apostles, heard their voices as they spoke to him, as they tried to cast the demon out, but there was no change to the shaking of his body. He was in his father's arms, but the movement continued.

Finally, with no success, his father left the apostles, and Sethe could sense the crowd all around him. Sethe could feel their eyes on him. He could sense their fear — their wondering thoughts.

And then a voice he recognized spoke:

"O faithless generation, how long shall I be with you? How long shall I suffer you? Bring him to me."

It was Jesus. But he could not see him. Everything was still dark.

"How long is it ago since this came to him?"

"Of a child. And ofttimes it hath cast him into the fire, and into the waters, to destroy him: but if thou canst do anything, have compassion on us, and help us." His father's voice!

"If thou canst believe, all things are possible to him that believeth," Jesus said.

And my father cried out, "Lord, I believe..."

There was a pause, and Sethe wondered again at the dream that had prepared him to accept this very moment. "Help thou mine unbelief."

"Thou dumb and deaf spirit, I charge thee, come out of him, and enter no more into him."

The darkness inside wrenched itself from his soul, and like a burst of sunlight, the power of God filled Sethe's veins, his skin, his eyes. He could feel the warmth of the Messiah's hands. A voice did not speak to him but he felt the words.

"Your soul is healed."

Sethe turned to his father, a man who never cried, and to his mother. She was with them.

It was indeed him. "I told you I would come," the Messiah said.

The Healing of the Ten Lepers – James Tissot, 1886-1894

One Leper

Luke 17

Micah had endured persecution for as long as he could remember. As a young child, his parents had died, and as a youth Micah had fallen prey to robbery, only to change his ways, work as a fisherman, and discover he was leprous.

Some said it was his sin of robbery that had caused it. He knew of others within the valley of Gehenna who had been afflicted in like manner because of lying, arrogance, envy, and idol worship, or so said the Rabbis. One of them, a friend named Asher, a Jew, had spent his days searching for God only to receive the same end.

"It came upon me suddenly," Asher said.

Micah had come to know others before Asher. Reuben, the only son of a sheepherder, Stephen, a carpenter, Joel, a potter. Damaris, a young married woman. She lived alone, without her family, for over five years before being pronounced clean.

Another woman much older, Mary by name, had burned her skin while cooking, only to have swelling appear the following day and a thin crust of skin and a whitish-red spot appear on her lower arm soon thereafter. Weeks later, her hair was falling out and turning a pale white. One of her children had followed after her, cursed with the same uncleanliness. And while she had been able to go home, going through the rituals prescribed by the priests, her child had remained in the valley of Gehenna just outside the city where he'd lived for only six months.

The sickness had affected many. A woman of long ago, Miriam by name, had suffered leprosy for a week because she had spoken against Moses and his choice of a wife – an Ethiopian woman. She was never sent out of the city because her cleansing had taken place quickly. But King Uzziah, who had been quarantined inside a separate chamber of his home, had never again left this chamber until the day of his death.

Micah knew of the pain. It was torturous, the itching terrible at first until the numbness entered in and he could not feel anything. The disfigurement was horrifying. Micah had not looked at himself in years not even when he'd gone to draw water from the lake of death.

For this reason, and others which were often spoken of in hushed tones, Micah had prayed that the uncleanliness would pass. It had been two years with Asher, and three more with him. Unfortunately for all of them, the priests had not cured a single leper. It was up to the individual to pray and fast. The priests, whether Jewish or Samaritan, could pronounce an individual clean, nothing more.

He had never seen the ceremonies of purification himself, but he had heard of them through the years. Cedarwood, a crimson cloth, and a live bird were dipped into a vessel of water holding the blood of a second bird, to rid the leper of his or her demonic disease. The leper, sprinkled with the water and blood mixture, went through the cleansing process seven times. The live bird was then set free.

The leper was then allowed into the city, where a physical cleansing took place. Clothing, mildewed, and full of putrid smells, was washed, hair was shaved, and a bath of cleansing was undertaken. Following the ritual, the leper waited another seven days, did not enter into his or her residence, and returned to Gehenna after performing the same ritual once again.

On the eighth day, he or she was allowed into the sanctuary. Oil was brought and a lamb for the offerings. Birds could be used instead of sheep for the whole and purification offerings if the leper came from a poor family. But for the meal and reparation offerings, only a lamb and log of oil could be used for purification.

Micah prayed that such a day would come for him.

He was tired, though grateful, for the food and water that Asher brought to him. He could no longer walk without help, and Asher was known to scavenge for not only the two of them but for others living in the outskirts of the city. Previous to living here, Asher had been charged with not keeping his promise to pay back his debtor, a wise man on the hill who had plenty for himself and most of the underlying population. Soon thereafter, leprosy had come to him.

A story from Micah's mother still kept him awake at night. That of Naaman, captain of the host of the king of Syria. A wealthy and mighty man, he yet had contracted leprosy despite all of his greatness. While speaking to a captive handmaiden in Samaria, he'd heard of a prophet of God who could cleanse him. Believing in her words, he'd traveled to the house of Elisha only to be told by Elisha's servant that to be clean he must wash in Jordan seven times. Naaman couldn't believe it. Wash? He had to go to a lowly river and wash? Abana and Pharpar were beautiful, clean rivers. Why tell him to go to Israelite water? And why have a mere servant tell him to go? Why not come out himself and cleanse him?

His mother's words still rang out, and tears filled Micah's eyes as he thought on the story that would soon mirror his own life, though he knew it not. Naaman had finally humbled himself. He'd looked beyond the fact that a servant had spoken to him, that he had to do something himself. Make an effort. He went and dipped himself seven times in the Jordan, because of the wise counsel of his servants. Thereby, the great man became clean.

"How is the food?" Asher asked.

Micah, who had been eating in silence, looked up.

"What is it?" he asked.

"Bread, I think." A wan smile.

His friend's face was barely distinguishable, rough, his eyes hollow.

"I am grateful."

"The water should be cleaner today. I went beyond the Jordan."

"Not a well?"

"It was near dark. No one saw me."

He drank. The water was clean.

"Thank you."

His friend nodded and returned to his food. After a time, he spoke again. "There is a man by the name of Jesus."

"I have heard of him."

"Then you know what he does."

"He speaks to the people."

"Yes. And he heals them. A woman of Samaria has met with him. She believes that he is the Messiah. It was at Jacob's Well that I took the water."

"It is good. And the Messiah?"

"I haven't been able to find him. But I hear he is coming. Talk is that he will be visiting Galilee."

"He is coming to Jerusalem?"

"Yes. He will be passing through Samaria."

"Why would he do that?"

"I don't know. But others tell me that this Jesus doesn't think like other men. He doesn't think or act like the rulers of the synagogues. They say he is God."

"Have you told the others he is coming?"

"No. I wanted to speak with you first. Do you think they will go with us?"

"To the village? Yes, but I cannot walk."

"We will help you."

"I don't know."

"It is time, I feel it. Something is going to happen, but we have to meet him. We must have faith."

"I am near death. I cannot walk."

His friend leaned closer. It was the first time he'd been so close. Micah almost cried out.

"I...can't."

"You can, and I and the others will help you."

"How many others?"

"As many as will go."

Micah wasn't a great man like Naaman, not even a rich man, but perhaps, with the help of the others, he could do this. The following morning, as a few of his friends approached – nine others – he thought of all of those, who, through faith in Jesus, had been healed.

Reuben, Stephen, and Joel stood near their friend. The other five were a blacksmith from Jerusalem, a scribe, a merchant, and two shepherds. All these had left their trades when pronounced unclean and had come to live in the hell called Gehenna.

And now they would return to the village that at one time they'd been accepted in.

The deterioration of their clothing evident, their faces and arms full of uncleanliness, their feet bare of constraints and pressure, they walked the few miles to the village. The wind was rough that day, the day Micah would always remember. His eyes burned from the sand, and as they approached the village, someone yelled:

"Lepers!"

It was a child's voice.

The air was hot as it whipped across Micah's face; hot and stinging, as the ten of them stood there – waiting. Jesus was there. Micah could not see him but there were people in the village, so many people, and they were looking up at them.

Oh, to be invisible! To be gone from their sight!

"I can't do this," Micah said.

"I have been told otherwise," answered Asher, pressing him even higher to his feet.

"My legs – hurt!"

"Look! It is Jesus. He is coming!"

Micah looked down the hill. A man was walking towards them. "Master!" he shouted. The others followed, shouting down the hill, "Jesus, have mercy on us!"

"Go shew yourselves unto the priests!" Jesus called back.

Something like a ray of light pierced Micah's soul. Leaning onto his friend they entered the village, the scoffing and scuffling of many filling his ears with fear – hate. The sound was like the roaring of lions and the howling of heavy wind. It was deafening, and once or twice Micah shut his eyes, thinking of his mother's story.

Then, suddenly, he was walking alone, unaided. Stopping, he looked down. His feet were clean! Looking down at his arms, he gasped. "Glory to God!" he cried, looking up at the skies. No one spoke. And his brethren, including Asher, were gone.

Micah turned. He could still see Him. He was a long distance away, but he could see him, like a light in a window, like a journey on a dark road.

"Jesus!"

He ran, though the running seemed to take forever. He was clean. Clean! Stopping at Jesus' feet he fell on his face. "Thank you, Master! Thank you!" he uttered.

The touch of the master's hand brought his head up.

"Were there not ten cleansed? But where are the nine?"

"I do not know."

"Arise, go thy way: thy faith hath made thee whole," Jesus said.

"My faith?" he answered.

In a blink, Micah remembered it all. Where he lived, up this very road; the wife he had known and loved for fifteen, no twenty years. His children. He had five. The oldest was ten. No, fifteen by now. Would they know him? Would they remember him? What would he say? Do?

It was a short walk to the priests. A short walk to the Temple Mount where he would be pronounced clean. And then, finally, he could go home.

The Blind Man at the Pool of Siloam – Edmund Blair Leighton, 1879

Bartimaeus' Sight
John 9

Bartimaeus was born blind. As a child, his hands were his eyes, his nose his compass to food. He loved to eat and brush his tiny hands through the grains of sand. He loved to feel his mother's face, smooth like a stone, soft like the fleece of a lamb. Her voice was quiet and still, like the waters of Galilee.

His father, Timaeus, had a different sort of face, strong and bearded. He had touched it, but only once that he could remember. His voice could be loud, filling the room of their home like a great wind, but lately, the storm had subsided. He was ten, and Mother was going to have a baby.

"Can I help you with that?" his father would ask his mother.

"Perhaps you should lie down. I'll take care of Bartimaeus," and they would go out, and Father would take him to the river. They would talk and he would play.

Sometimes Father would talk about the water resources in Jerusalem, and Bartimaeus would listen to his words. There were wells that people drew from, and springs, channels, and pools.

The Pool of Siloam was his mother's favorite place other than the temple. It stood at the end of Hezekiah's rock tunnel. Almost seven centuries ago, a limestone water channel had been carved by hand. It was long and hid the Gihon spring which led to the pool, from those who gave reverence to Sennacherib, king of Assyria. It remained hidden during the war and was never found by its enemies. Mother called it her Living Water.

When Bartimaeus returned home from his time alone with Father, his mother would be rested, and she would tell him about the coming of the Messiah to the world. She would remind him of the law and would relate the story of ancient Israel escaping bondage, and their loving redemption, as if she had actually been there.

"It is called the Feast of the Tabernacles," she would often tell him in those days before the baby was born. "And we will be outdoors in our branch laden Sukkot for seven days, eating and sleeping to remember the Israelites wandering in the wilderness for forty years."

Leah was born, and she was perfectly formed. She could see and run and not trip or run into things. As she grew older, she would take him by the hand and show him places his eyes could not see. He would feel the water, and she would teach him about God.

Years later, when he was almost thirty, he neared the temple in Jerusalem. There were many people there that day, and he could hear the voices around him snapping and cracking like locusts. Inside the Treasury, where the money for the poor was given, and giant lampstands, seventy-feet high stood to give light to the temple, he heard, "I am the light of the world: he that followeth me shall not walk in darkness but shall have the light of life" (John 8:12).

Though Bartimaeus had never seen light he imagined what it would be like – warm and bright – and the height of the lampstands that must have reached into heaven.

This had to be Jesus. He had heard him twice before, and Bartimaeus was struck with awe at his words. He had followed Jesus since his experience at the mountain – but the Pharisees were angry. As he listened, Jesus said, "And ye shall know the truth, and the truth shall make you free" (John 8:32).

A warmth like the sun shining fell upon Bartimaeus' face. Yes, this was light, and perhaps one day he would see. Someone brushed past him. "You should not be here," he said.

The voice was that of a boy, but the boy had already left him. Anger filled the courtyard of the temple. It was the last day of the Feast of the Tabernacles, and, as Bartimaeus listened, he realized that not even his father had been so angry with God. Once Leah had been born, perfect, and healthy, his father had never returned to his yelling ways.

He continued to listen, even though many others brushed past him. He was kicked and spat upon. Money was dropped in front of him – coins he did not gather. Didn't the people know the coins were to be placed in the trumpet-shaped boxes and not in front of his feet? He remained still and continued to listen.

"He that is of God heareth my words: ye therefore hear them not, because ye are not of God."

Feeling for the wall, slick, and cold at his touch, Bartimaeus attempted to walk closer so he could hear more clearly. In an instant, he was pushed to the ground. His hands burned from the fall. He brushed them quickly against his lips. "Move!" a man shouted.

Leaving the Treasury entrance, he crept and felt his way to the wall he knew so well. It was a quiet spot. He had received money there. He had received pity. He sat. The wall was thick behind him, the stones smooth at his touch. Beyond the wall was the path leading to the Pool of Siloam.

Could he travel alone? Down myriad steps and through the heat and busyness of the day?

He had reached the temple from his home; could he do the same to the pool? But he must.

Within minutes, others had found him.

They stopped. For a moment, all was silent. He could feel eyes on him. Was he in the way of the last morning procession to the waters where a priest would draw water from the pool into the golden pitcher and return the water to the temple to end the last day of the feast? It was mid-morning; he could feel the beginning of heat on his cheeks. Hadn't this ritual already been accomplished? Or were the priests returning from the pool with the pitcher to the temple, so that God would bless them with rain for the coming year?

Perhaps they were looking at his soiled clothing, his bruised hands? Would they care about him now?

"Will you take me to the pool?" he asked.

Someone laughed.

"It is a long walk when one is blind," he offered hopefully.

Someone took his hand. "Brother, what are you doing?" she asked.

"Sister, is that you?"

"Who else? Where are you going?"

"To the pool of Siloam. Can you take me?"

"Of course. But these men are looking at you strangely. I don't think they want you to go."

"When has that ever been a problem for me?"

Leah laughed.

"I'll take you as far as the outer Siloam wall. Mother needs me."

"That will do."

Taking his arm, she led him for some time. He could hear the others speaking of Jesus; not all of the words were pleasant. Leah spoke to him often, sharing with him her plans for the future, her plans for the present – would she need to return for him so that he might eat supper with them? And as the heat became almost too unbearable, his feet bruised and hot, she stopped.

"There. The wall is there."

She placed his hand on the smooth stone of the pool of Siloam.

"I will see you soon."

He nodded. She would see the gesture even though he knew not how she looked at him as she left. But he knew she loved him. He knew that.

Sitting at the wall he took a few minutes to breathe deeply. He was tired. And thirsty. Well, his thirst would be quenched soon. And then he heard it; words that appeared to be spoken to him.

"Who did sin, this man, or his parents, that he was born blind?" a man asked.

Had his parents sinned? It was a question he'd thought of often. Had they? He knew little about the life before this one, though he had heard his parents speak of the possibility more than once of a pre-mortal life.

"Neither hath this man sinned, nor his parents: but that the works of God should be made manifest in him. I must work the works of him that sent me, while it is day: the night cometh, when no man can work. As long as I am in the world, I am the light of the world."

There was a slight movement of feet, a silence as something seemed to be gathered. A warm hand was placed at his cheek. He was startled, but only for a moment. He could not breathe. A coolness on his eyelids followed, an anointing and a tender hand at his back directed him up.

"Go, wash in the pool of Siloam. I send thee."

Jesus?

115

There were many steps to the water. But it was unlike Bartimaeus to deny a hopeful word even if it wasn't Jesus. He began. As he descended, he could feel the silence wrap around him and through him. The sweet smell of palms and the sound of bees spoke to him of the future. All was quiet other than this, and his footsteps to the water, and yet, he knew others were nearby. He knew he was not alone.

Reaching the base of the steps, the cool water reached his toes. Slowly, reverently, he stepped down. When the water reached his waist, he stopped. Even the water was still. Reaching his hands into the coolness, he cupped his hands, and, bringing his hands to his face, rinsed his eyes.

The coolness dripped from his face, and for a moment his eyes remained closed.

Slowly, he opened them.

He had never seen color before, or shapes, though he'd felt them; the shape of faces and hands and arms as he'd struggled to find the market, his home, his bed. It was like he imagined seeing to be. Bright. Warm. Friendly.

He looked at his hands, turned them, like a special cloth, memorizing all of the rising and falling of his veins, bones, and skin, like the rising and falling of stitches in a sacred garment.

He looked up.

Jesus. He was at the top of the steps, looking down at him. He stood with the others, and yet, alone, his garments plain yet beautiful. His eyes were bright and searching. His hands at his sides.

Bartimaeus walked up the steps he had just recently descended, smelling and tasting the sights he'd experienced on the way down to the waters, enjoying the textures, the colors, the warmth. At the top of the wall, the exact place where Jesus had stood and directed him to descend, he looked for him.

Instead, a man pushed him and asked, "Are you not he that sat and begged?"

"I am he."

"He is like him," a woman said.

"How are thine eyes opened?" another asked.

They surrounded him like bees to honey.

"A man that is called Jesus made clay, and anointed mine eyes, and said unto me, 'Go to the pool of Siloam, and wash': and I went and washed and received sight."

"Where is he?" the woman asked.

"I know not."

Hands reached out – cruel hands. People he did not know pulled him as he walked back to the temple. Just like before, it took some time. And just like before, the stares did not matter. He enjoyed the scene before him and dreamt of the moment he would see his parents and sister again.

As Bartimaeus approached the Temple Mount he could only gasp. It was large and more impressive than even his most vivid dreams had produced. For the first time, he saw with his own eyes the cloisters or covered walkways that opened to the inside courts, and the double row of columns cut from stone. Yes, they indeed reached the heavens. Bartimaeus tried to breathe. He tried to walk without tripping. He did not want to miss a thing!

Towers of light stone, shining pillars, high windows, and a thick, glowing door met his eyes. So these were the temple doors. He could see them through the Nicanor Gate and Court of the Men of Israel. There, there was the altar and the place of sacrifice. People, so many people. Colors. So many colors!

He blinked. It was the sabbath day, and what a glorious day it was!

"How did you receive your sight?" a man asked. He blinked from the awesome scene and turned. A Pharisee?

The man wore a dark robe with a light shawl on his head – the same darkness was sewn in dark and light near the bottom. On his forehead was a tefillah. Shaped like a box, the tefillin was held by a strap and wrapped around his forehead. Inside the tefillin were verses from the Torah used for prayer.

Others had followed him and stood nearby.

"He put clay upon mine eyes, and I washed, and do see."

The Pharisee turned to his companions. "This man is not of God, because he keepeth not the sabbath day."

"How can a man that is a sinner do such miracles?" asked another man dressed in similar attire. He could feel the anger erupting even before he saw it in the eyes in front of him. It was almost as before when he could only hear.

Turning to him, the Pharisee asked again, "What sayest thou of him, that he hath opened thine eyes?"

"He is a prophet."

"We do not believe that you were blind and received your sight. Call his parents!"

They did not *believe?*

Still, Bartimaeus' heart skipped a beat as he thought again about his parents! As he stood in the place of reverence and devotion to God, he knew that all would be made right. All had to be made right. He had been healed by Jesus and he could never deny the truth.

Time moved slowly as he waited. He listened to the breathing of the others, watched the skies as they spoke of the Son that came

I Walked With Jesus

down from heaven. Watched the people. How different they all were!

But when they came through the Court of the Women, he knew. Running to them, he embraced them. "Oh, Father! Mother!" he sang. His mother's skin, once soft and warm, was lined cruelly through years of labor. His father's strong voice shook as he spoke to him. "Oh – my – son!" But they were here – here!

"Is this your son, who ye say was born blind? How doth he now see?"

His mother looked on him kindly. Though old age had come to her, she was yet beautiful.

"We know that this is our son," she said evenly. "And that he was born blind. But by what means he now seeth, we know not; or who hath opened his eyes, we know not: he is of age; ask him: he shall speak for himself."

There was a pause, and Bartimaeus reflected on the gift he had been given.

"Give God the praise: we know that this man is a sinner," said the first Pharisee.

"Whether he be a sinner or no, I know not: one thing I know, that, whereas I was blind, now I see," Bartimaeus said.

"What did he to thee? How opened he thine eyes?"

"I have told you already, and ye did not hear: wherefore would ye hear it again? Will ye also be his disciples?"

Bartimaeus was amazed at their lack of understanding. Yet, perhaps, they only wished to follow Jesus.

"No! Don't you see? He is an evil man! And thou art his disciple; but we are Moses' disciples. We know that God spake unto Moses: as for this fellow, we know not from whence he is."

They did not *know*?

"Why herein is a marvelous thing, that you know not from whence he is, and yet he hath opened mine eyes," he began as they stared at him, their mouths gaping. "Now we know that God heareth not sinners: but if any man be a worshipper of God, and doeth his will, him he heareth. Since the world began was it not heard that any man opened the eyes of one that was born blind – except he be of God? If this man were not of God, he could do nothing."

The foremost Pharisee continued to stare at him. He did not blink.

"Thou wast altogether born in sin, and dost thou teach *us*?"

It seemed impossible, not after all he'd experienced, not after all he knew, that he could be removed from the temple court. But with a wave of the second Pharisee's arm, Bartimaeus was removed. Within seconds he was outside the temple gate.

Lifting his head, he walked around the outer gate to the east. The sun warmed his face just like it had always done, but, this time, he couldn't look at it directly. The sun burned. Still, he knew it was there, just as he knew Jesus had saved him from the darkness.

There was a man who waited. He looked as if he would speak to him.

"Dost thou believe on the Son of God?" Though he wore simple clothes; his eyes spoke a thousand words.

"Who is he, Lord, that I might believe on him?"

"Thou hast both seen him, and it is he that talketh with thee."

Truly? Bartimaeus fell to the earth. He bowed before him. Yes, he knew this voice. And now, he knew this face.

"Lord, I believe," he said. The tears were fresh, the heartache real. He could see everything now, including the Pharisees who had also come out to speak with him.

120

"For judgment I am come into this world," Jesus said, placing his right hand on Bartimaeus' shoulder, "that they which see not might see; and that they which see might be made blind."

Bartimaeus stood.

"Are we blind also?" the first Pharisee asked.

"If ye were blind, ye should have no sin: but now ye say, 'We see; therefore, your sin remaineth.'"

Jesus touched Bartimaeus's cheek. His eyes spoke again, telling him truths the others would one day see. Bartimaeus thanked him, his dark eyes filling with tears.

Slowly, thoughtfully, he made his way home.

The Miracle of the Loaves and the Fishes – Bartolome
EstebanMurillo, 1617 – 1682

Fisher Boy
John 6

Nathan had been a fisher boy as far back as he could remember. He was only seven, and it seemed to him, he could remember playing at the water's edge at three – either that, or he was remembering the stories his mother and father always told him about himself.

He had one older brother and one older sister, and his father was a fisherman by trade. His father smelled fishy most nights, but that mattered little. It was enough to see the fish accompanying him home in the cart.

His father was strong, and many said his mother was delicate and beautiful. He just thought his mother kind. It was she that tucked him in bed at night, made a proper supper, and never forgot to call him Fisher Boy.

When Father was out, she was home. And when his brother and sister would get noisy, he'd dream of the nighttime when his mother would read him to sleep.

She knew all of the stories. Noah and the ark. Daniel and the lions. Jonah and the whale. And he would ask for them over and over.

When Jesus came, she would take him to hear his stories. His father would come when he could, and his brother and sister would watch the Master wide-eyed as he told about the grain of mustard seed, the treasure hidden in the field, and the first commandment – to love God.

During these times, Nathan's mind and heart filled with awe and wonder.

When Nathan was almost eight, his mother grew ill. Instead of telling him stories at night, she spent her time in bed and Nathan's sister, Miriam, took care of him. She was bossy, and rarely remembered to tell him stories. At night, his father's time would turn to Mother. They would talk and remember the good times.

One day, while his sister, Miriam, was preparing the daily bread for the family, Nathan watched. It wasn't like him to watch, but there was something about today that made him want to look. His mother was still sick, no doctors had been able to cure her, but there was a feeling in the home that made him wonder about the bread. And so, he did.

"Go out and play," his sister demanded. "You're hanging over the dough."

Nathan ignored her and watched. Some of the ingredients he knew. Salt. Olive oil. Wheat flour. He watched Miriam grind it and blow off its husk, and now it was being kneaded. Other flours had been added to the mix: barley, broad bean, millet, and lintel, but telling the differences between them had always been difficult. Some beans were almost white, others were a light yellow, and one of them had white and yellow together before being ground into powder. They were different sizes too, though always small.

Nathan smiled over at the dough that would soon be kneaded into five flat, round loaves and cooked on coals until brown. But for now, as his sister had left the baking area, all he could do was look down at them and remember their taste just out of the oven.

Two hours later the dough mounds were ready.

Nathan watched as his sister placed the loaves on the coals and cooked them. It didn't take long, but the waiting seemed like forever. Yes, there was something about today, though he didn't know what.

He waited, thinking of his mother who lay in bed though it was mid-day. His father would be home soon and they would all gather around the table to eat and talk. His mother might even join them if she felt well enough.

Nathan was in this mindset when the bread was removed from the coals. His father walked in with the morning's catch, and his brother, Paul, raced to see how many fish he'd caught.

Two, exactly two, and they were small.

Father shrugged his shoulders and smiled. "The bread smells heavenly," he said. "It will suffice."

Mother was suddenly leaning against the high archway of the kitchen, and she was smiling too. "I feel much better today," she said, though her skin looked pale, and Nathan could tell she needed something to drink.

"Thirsty?" he asked her.

"How did you know, Fisher Boy?"

Nathan ran, retrieved a cup from the shelf, poured the water from their only pitcher, and returned the cup to his mother who was now sitting, along with the rest of them, at the table.

"I want to see Jesus today," she said. "Perhaps we can eat there."

"With all of this?" Father said, laughing. Nathan was unsure of what he meant.

"I'm serious," Mother said, looking into the eyes of her children. She looked tired, and Nathan wondered how well she was actually doing. "I have felt impressed with the Spirit to find Jesus and spend some time hearing his voice. Who will join me?"

"We can take the five loaves," Mother said. "And *all* of the fish."

Father laughed.

Shutting the door behind them, the family of five, walked together. As Nathan's sandaled feet stepped through the dusty lanes, he tried to remember what was happening today. The place where they lived was buzzing with talk. He listened to his parents, his brother, and sister, but nothing made sense, nothing except that something terrible had happened, something frightening that was spoken about in whispers.

"How could they kill him?" Miriam asked.

"How could they chop off –" Paul began.

His father held up his hand to silence his oldest son.

"What did they chop off?" Nathan asked.

There was silence in the air, and then his mother spoke.

"John the Baptist was killed today."

"The prophet? When?" Nathan asked. John the Baptist was a good man. He'd baptized his father and mother, his brother and sister.

"Early this morning," his father replied.

"Are we going to his burial, first?" Nathan asked.

"No," his father answered.

"We are going to hear Jesus, Fisher Boy," his mother said, touching his cheek.

Father and Mother exchanged glances.

"See the people?" instructed his mother.

Nathan looked again. The streets were filled; a mass of people walking to the sea. There were too many for Nathan to count, and they filled the roads as far as the eye could see.

"Remember all of the miracles of Jesus?" his mother asked.

"I remember." His sister, Miriam, wrapped her slim arm around her mother. "Is that why we are going, so that you might be healed?" she asked.

Mother was silent. When she spoke again, her voice was strong.

"Jesus will be at the mountain."

They continued to walk, the air hot and biting. Nathan's feet were beginning to hurt but he didn't complain. They had also brought along a goatskin bag of water, and he knew there would be a moment of refreshment before the food was passed out while they listened to Jesus.

He tried to think of the stories of Jesus he had most enjoyed, the stories he'd been told by his mother at night before the terrible sickness had come upon her; a sickness that weakened her bones and made it difficult for her to stand for long periods, though today, she appeared to be doing well.

The noise of feet shuffling, and voices speaking, was strong now that they were with the group, working their way to the Sea of Galilee.

"There must be thousands," Father said.

Mother nodded. She smiled, and a single tear wet her cheek.

By the time the family stopped, the air had cooled some, it was getting late. The family sat.

"How will we hear him from way back here?" Nathan asked.

"Drink some water, Fisher Boy," his mother invited, and in moments each family member had taken a sip or two, and the bag was going around for a second turn.

Jesus was so far away. He was a tiny dot in the distance. Nathan could see him and the apostles, but he could not hear what they were saying. The people were sitting down, as Nathan and his family had done. As Nathan wondered when Jesus would speak, he felt the presence of someone at his side. Looking up he saw a man.

Jesus!

Jesus squatted beside him. He looked into his eyes, and then up into the eyes of his mother sitting by him. "I am glad you have come," he said.

"Mother is sick," Nathan said.

"And she has come all this way," Jesus said.

His mother sniffed behind him.

"Yes," Nathan said.

A tender hand brushed the hair from his eyes. "Then it is time," Jesus said.

Nathan closed his eyes. He listened to the prayer. When Jesus was finished, he stood and left them. Nathan watched him walk to an old woman and speak with her. He saw him bless the woman. Jesus went to a man. He placed his hands on his head. Then he got up and went to someone else. Jesus blessed a child. As he made his way to the front of the group, he spoke to his apostles. Nathan could not hear him.

He touched his mother's hand. It was warm and her face was bright and glowing. She no longer looked sick. Tears that had found her eyes had wetted her clothing. Father was holding her, and her brother and sister had clasped hands.

There was never such a day as this.

There was movement above him. Nathan looked up. A man he recognized was smiling down at him.

"Hello, boy. My name is Andrew. I see you have loaves in that basket."

"Barley loaves. And fish!"

"How many fish?"

"Two. They are small." He opened the basket he'd been carrying.

"Jesus needs them."

Nathan looked at his mother. She said something with her eyes. He looked at his father. And then at his brother and sister. Everyone was silent.

The feeling he'd had since the time he'd awoken was still there. The same feeling he'd felt as Jesus had blessed his mother. Peace.

Nathan lifted the basket of bread and retrieved the fish from his basket. Placing the fish on top, he handed the basket up.

Andrew thanked him and walked to the front of the crowd where Jesus stood. They were on a high hill, but still in a desert place, and they were so far away. But suddenly, the voice of Jesus was heard. Jesus was blessing the food.

Time passed. When the basket arrived for Nathan and his family, it still had bread and fish in it. Nathan looked around. Everyone was eating. Everyone!

He looked at his mother. She was crying again. His father was silent. His brother and sister had plenty of food in front of them. They were eating. He looked down at the basket. There were – what? Ten loaves and one-two-three… 15 fish!

"It's a miracle," his mother said.

"A miracle," his father answered, touching her hand.

Christ Healing the Ear of Malchus – Louis Finson, 1600 – 1630

Malchus' Word
John 8 & 18

From the days of his birth, Malchus had learned about the importance of words. How words gave information to the seeker, how they helped with tasks, and if you listened, how they gave direction in one's life path.

Now that he was twelve, Malchus was giving greater thought to his father's employ. What he did. What he said. What his father expected him to do.

Though neither Malchus nor his father had been allowed inside the Court of the Priests at the Temple Mount, his father had spoken often of the duties therein. Even his father was kept from places he would never be able to guard even though he was an Israelite. Not even the altar where animals were sacrificed was open to him. He could stand as close as Nicanor Gate and the Court of the Men of Israel, fifteen steps up, but could go no further.

When his father spoke about the Sanctuary or the Holy of Holies where only the Priests could enter, a strange light burned within his eyes. There was something to that place that couldn't be spoken. But his father knew about the two columns so named Jachin and Boaz – like Solomon's Temple – and the veil leading to the Holy of Holies.

More times than he could count, since his induction, his father had watched the Captain of the Temple Guard raise his torch with the embers burning like a glowing jewel.

"O officer of the Temple Mount, peace be to thee!" the captain would shout. If the officer didn't stir – being asleep – the captain would light the guard on fire. He would scream, awaken, and roll on the ground, his tunic burning wild with orange heat. Sometimes the captain would strike a head or two with the end of his staff.

The first time Malchus heard the story, he cried.

"It is a brave, important thing to be a Temple Guard," his mother had said, and Malchus wondered at her words.

Later, Malchus' father was made Captain of the Temple Guard. He was second-in-command to the High Priest, Caiaphas, and had full command of the guard.

Malchus was proud of him. He wanted to be like him. He wanted to be strong and brave. "Watch at the Chamber of Stone!" his father would tell him. "Watch at the Chamber of the Hearth. Watch..."

It was on such a day when his father was at work that Malchus first saw the boy called Jesus. Malchus often followed his father to the Temple Mount and waited at the outer gates, moving frequently so as not to be discovered by his father.

That day, Jesus was sitting in the Court of the Women. He could see him from the front pillars, near the entrance of Beautiful Gate. He knew what happened in there. He'd heard talk of it in the streets. The lepers went inside to be seen by the priests, and the Jewish women could go so far as the Nicanor Gate which led to the Court of the Men of Israel. Near the wood store, where Nazarites would prepare their special sacrifices, he'd heard the voice of Jesus with his own ears.

The boy was teaching… something. It was Passover, the time of remembrance when God had smitten the firstborn of the Egyptians. The Jews were passed over because of the lamb's blood that was sprinkled on the lintel and side posts of the doors of their houses. It was a strange thing to Malchus, like burning a man's clothes when he was asleep.

But at the wood store, he listened.

The boy was preaching. He was full of wisdom, only he wasn't old, about his age he guessed. There were old men, chief priests, captains of the guards, women, children, and elders, listening, filling the air with grunts and silence.

And then he saw them – a man and a woman. They looked worried. They flew past him, hardly seeing him.

He could not hear their voices. But Jesus stood and walked with them to the gate.

"Son, why hast thou thus dealt with us? Thy father and I have sought thee sorrowing."

"How is it that ye sought me?" Jesus answered. "Wist ye not that I must be about my Father's business?"

Malchus knew that Jesus' father's business was in carpentry. But that wasn't what he was doing now. He was teaching. What father could he mean?

"Son, what are you doing?"

Malchus looked up to see his father's face. Dirt lined the furrows of his thick brows. His eyes looked angry.

"What about you, Father? Have you been building something for Caiaphas?" he asked solemnly.

"No, son, I have been searching for you, in all of the hiding places you like to go."

He shrugged. "I am here as you can see."

"Your mother is in sorrow." He took Malchus by the arm. "What have I told you about spending time here? This is not a place for children."

Malchus might have argued, he had seen a few children here, but something in his father's tone told him to remain silent. "You can release me. I will go to Mother," he said.

It was a short walk to his hillside home, and once there he watched as his mother baked. She was always cooking something good. His family, unlike others, always had plenty to eat – egg, fish, fruit, bread. The pebble floor clapped against his sandals as he walked toward her.

"Mother!"

"Malchus. So, you've been at the Temple Mount again."

"How did you know?" Malchus smiled. He couldn't help it. Mother and Father believed in God, in the heavenly place after death, but it was his mother who usually spoke to him about spiritual things. It was she who had taught him how to pray, and she who believed in the rituals of God, even though his father was the one who was allowed beyond the Nicanor Gate – closest to the Court of the High Priests, and the Court of the Men of Israel, though no further.

Time passed and Malchus continued to learn from his mother about God, and his father, about how to serve the people as a Temple Guard. It was no surprise then, when eight years later, and he was twenty, Malchus was inducted into duty. He did not love the position as he thought he would, but he enjoyed spending time with his father, and that sufficed. Ten years later, however, he was thirty and his father had passed on.

There was great mourning in the city that day, mourning that Malchus would never forget. His father had been a great man. Though stern at times, he had protected the Temple Mount with skill and reverence. Malchus knew his father's strength had never come from God, at least not completely. He knew his father trusted in his own strength, his own courage. But even so, Malchus had learned. Even at a young age, he'd had thoughts about his strength coming from somewhere else.

When he was called by Ananus – father-in-law to Caiaphas – to take his father's place, Malchus took on the role of Captain of the Temple Guard with outward ease. But he did not enjoy it, especially now. Without his father, the Temple Mount seemed hollow, the southern portico not so grand as he'd once thought it. Everywhere he stood as a guard, whether it was at the Susa Gate, the outer court, or the balustrade – the place of warning for Gentiles not to enter – he thought of Jesus and the fisherman he had called.

Oh, to be one of them!

Unlike his father who had reveled in the job pronounced upon him, Malchus dreamed of the days he could return and listen to Jesus.

One year passed, and when Malchus was thirty-one, he made a pilgrimage to the Temple Mount. It was the time of Passover once again, and thoughts of peace entered his mind and heart as he thought about Jesus. Malchus had not yet married. It was enough to take care of his mother. She was ill. Would Jesus have something to say to fill his hollow heart?

He traveled the short distance from the hillside to the Temple Mount and entered the outer court, spear in hand. He had assigned to himself the Treasury.

"How knoweth this man letters, having never learned?" someone was asking.

"My doctrine is not mine, but his that sent me," Jesus answered. "If any man will do his will, he shall know of the doctrine, whether it be of God, or whether I speak of myself. He that speaketh of himself seeketh his own glory: but he that seeketh his glory that sent him, the same is true, and no unrighteousness is in him. Did not Moses give you the law, and yet none of you keepeth the law? Why go ye about to kill me?"

The Treasury filled with voices. And suddenly, as if the earth had shifted, an angry voice Malchus didn't recognize shouted: "Thou hast a devil: who goeth about to kill thee?"

"Is not this he, whom they seek to kill? But, lo, he speaketh boldly, and they say nothing unto him," said another. "Do the rulers know indeed that this is the very Christ? Howbeit we know this man whence he is: but when Christ cometh, no man knoweth whence he is."

"Ye both know me, and ye know whence I am," Jesus cried. "I am not come of myself, but he that sent me is true, whom ye know not. But I know him: for I am from him, and he hath sent me."

The loudness grew, and this time many of the priests stood, shouting their hateful words. Malchus's heart pounded. Would they take Jesus?

"When Christ cometh, will he do more miracles than these which this man hath done?" someone shouted over the noise.

Suddenly Malchus was pushed forward. "You're the captain, do something about this!" one of them hissed. Seeing his hesitation, guards, lower than his rank, brushed past him and to the front. He did the same. But he did not touch Jesus, and neither did any of the others. Many in the group were still murmuring when Jesus stopped them. He didn't use his fists. Only his words.

"Yet a little while am I with you, and then I go unto him that sent me. Ye shall seek me, and shall not find me: and where I am, thither you cannot come."

There was another rumbling of words from the chief priests, and for a moment, Malchus wondered where the place he spoke of was. And then he remembered heaven. But questions were filling the space, making it difficult to think.

"Whither will he go, that we shall not find him? Will he go unto the dispersed among the Gentiles, and teach the Gentiles?"

"What manner of saying is that that he said, 'Ye shall seek me, and shall not find me: and where I am thither ye cannot come?'"

Jesus' words lingered, and by the last day of the feast, Malchus had already decided to return to the Temple Mount and hear the final words. There was something about them that wouldn't leave his heart. When they came, he was covered in a warm fire even warmer than the one inside his home or the one he had often sat around during guard duty.

Malchus drew within the Treasury. There were many men, priests mostly, but others graced the Court of the Women this day including women and children.

"If any man thirst, let him come unto me, and drink."

A chill, like those received when the time of the day was early, felt its way up Malchus' back.

"He that believeth on me, as the scripture hath said, out of his belly shall flow rivers of living water."

Malchus had felt the living water many times.

"Of a truth this is the Prophet," said a man sitting on the ground below him as he stood, guarding the assembly. Jesus' eyes turned to the man, and in a moment of breath, Malchus could feel Jesus' eyes on him.

"Yes. Of a truth!" A woman's voice towards the back of the group spoke. Jesus's eyes turned to the woman.

"This man is a prophet!"

"This is the Christ!"

"...Shall Christ come out of Galilee? Hath not the scripture said, 'Christ cometh of the seed of David, and out of the town of Bethlehem, where David was?'"

Shouts erupted once again and as Malchus turned his eyes to Jesus to discover what he would say, he was met by blue and penetrating eyes that seemed undisturbed by the shouting. There was a division between the believers and the unbelievers but Jesus was as calm as the early morning hours.

Behind him, chief priests and Pharisees had gathered.

"Why have you not brought him?" a Pharisee asked.

"Never man spake like this man," Malchus offered.

"Are you also deceived?" asked the Pharisee.

"Have any of the rulers or of the Pharisees believed on him?" asked a sitting petitioner.

"But this people who knoweth not the law are cursed," offered yet another listener.

"Doth our law judge any man, before it hear him, and know what he doeth?" asked Nicodemus, a Pharisee and ruler of the Jews, who was standing directly to Malchus' right.

"Art thou also of Galilee?" a voice shouted through the room. "Search and look: for out of Galilee ariseth no prophet."

Suddenly the room was silent. And in moments, those who had come to hear or curse him were standing and returning to their homes. Malchus remained standing until Jesus and his disciples were no longer in the Treasury. He waited until the women and children had left the Court of the Women.

What had happened here? Who was this Jesus that made his heart burn?

The twelve were with Jesus the next morning. Malchus had given himself the same duty. Like the day before, many had come to listen, and often, the show of anger would interfere with the words Jesus had to say.

As it was, this morning, just as Malchus entered the main hall, a young woman was being dragged into the center of the Court of the Women. She was screaming and weeping bitterly. Malchus remembered the days soon after his father's death. His mother had done the same, though there was something about the manner of this woman. She was afraid.

"Please!" she screamed, as a Pharisee known to Malchus, pushed her to the ground. Three scribes, one of which he also knew, looked on.

"This woman was taken in adultery, in the very act. Now Moses in the law commanded us, that such should be stoned: but what sayest thou?"

Jesus was silent. With his head bowed to the earth, he wrote with his finger on the ground.

"Well, what say ye?"

He continued to write. Malchus wondered why he did not speak.

"Should we stone her?"

The word 'stone' entered Malchus' heart. He stood still, hardly breathing. He was a Captain of the Temple guard, but he could not move.

Suddenly, Jesus lifted his head. "He that is without sin among you, let him first cast a stone at her."

The words entered with great force into Malchus' heart.

Jesus bowed his head once more and continued to write on the ground.

That's when Malchus felt it. He had to leave. And it had to be now.

Turning his back on the scene he watched others leaving just as he had done, from the oldest to the youngest among them, until Jesus and the woman were alone. Even the twelve had removed themselves, though Malchus could see them near the Nicanor Gate as before.

Jesus lifted his head. He said something. Malchus couldn't hear it.

The woman reached for him, weeping. Jesus of Nazareth held her, and for moments uncalculated in Malchus' mind, he watched the scene, his heart burning.

Then Jesus stood and walked with the woman. Malchus thought of his mother and the comfort Jesus would have given her if only she'd wanted to come with him today. But his mother was not strong in body, and the walk would have been difficult.

It was much later in the day when Malchus would find Jesus again at the same spot, surrounded by the angry, the curious, and the wondering.

"I am the light of the world: he that followeth me shall not walk in darkness, but shall have the light of life."

Mumbling erupted from the Pharisees. "Thou bearest record of thyself; thy record is not true."

"Though I bear record of myself, yet my record is true: for I know whence I came, and whither I go; but ye cannot tell whence I come, and whither I go. Ye judge after the flesh; I judge no man. And yet if I judge, my judgment is true: for I am not alone, but I and my Father that sent me. It is also written in your law, that the testimony of two men is true. I am one that bears witness of myself, and the Father that sent me beareth witness of me."

"Where is thy Father?"

"Ye neither know me, nor my Father: if ye had known me, ye should have known my Father also."

Anger swept across the room like a great wind, but no man touched Jesus.

"I go my way, and ye shall seek me, and shall die in your sins: whither I go, ye cannot come.

"Will he kill himself, because he saith, Wither I go, ye cannot come?"

"Ye are from beneath; I am from above: ye are of this world; I am not of this world."

The word *heaven* came back into Malchus' mind and his heart was warmed.

"I said therefore unto you, that ye shall die in your sins: for if ye believe not that I am he, ye shall die in your sins."

"Who art thou?"

"Even the same that I said unto you from the beginning. I have many things to say and to judge of you: but he that sent me is true; and I speak to the world those things which I have heard of him."

"What do you mean?" someone shouted. Malchus couldn't believe it. He knew who had sent Jesus. There was no doubt.

"When ye have lifted up the Son of man, then shall you know that I am he, and that I do nothing of myself; but as my Father hath taught me, I speak these things. And he that sent me is with me. The Father hath not left me alone; for I do always those things that please him."

Malchus did not understand what Jesus meant by being lifted up, but he did know that the healer had a father, just like he had a father – a father in heaven. There was no denying this. He looked around the room. There were tears in the eyes of some of the Jews; others were nodding their heads in agreement.

"If you continue in my word, then are ye my disciples indeed; and ye shall know the truth, and the truth shall make you free."

Malchus turned from the Treasury. He would have to move along. At the Nicanor Gate, he paused, and for a moment, listened. Nothing but the smell of blood and the bleating of sheep met his nose and ears. He climbed the steps and read the stone railing: "No Gentile shall enter inward of the partition and barrier surrounding the Temple, and whosover is caught shall be responsible to himself for his subsequent death" (3).

He would not enter the Court of the Men today but the words reminded him of what it would mean to any Gentile who forgot. It was capital punishment, and he would be the one to initiate their death.

The opposite of death was Truth. Could truth actually set a person free?

Thinking of the Master's words, Malchus returned home for a time to see his mother. She was waiting for him, as always, with food on the table. He wished she understood his heart, and there were moments when Malchus thought she did, and then the next day it was as if they'd never spoken of truth.

But today, as he spoke on the Master his mother's eyes wetted with tears. "What shall we do?" she asked.

"We follow him," he answered.

"But the others of our faith...they will not understand. You will lose your high position."

Malchus had thought of this possibility many times, but tonight he wondered even more about his mother's words. She was right. There would come a time when he'd have to speak out.

"We must follow him in our hearts – for now," Malchus said.

The following day the talk in the streets was that stones had been lifted against Jesus after he'd pronounced himself older than Abraham. Stones were lifted, but he had hidden somehow from the blows and had left the Treasury.

Many of them, including the chief priests and Pharisees, had understood little of his words. Perhaps this was to be expected, thought Malchus. Jesus spoke differently than anyone else he knew. It was almost like he spoke in tales or stories, and those who wanted to know the truth of his words would have to have an open heart to hear them.

Yes! That was it! That's how the truth made a person free!

The day after, Malchus returned to his work, only to hear other guards speak rudely of what they had heard the day before. He remained silent as he assisted in the watch of the Temple Mount for another day. Whether he was in the outer court or inside the Court of the Women, or merely in the Court of the Gentiles outside the Balustrade and Chamber of Hewn Stone, Malchus' feelings were the same. Only when he heard the words of the Master did he feel anything good coming from a place his people often called the house of God.

A year came and went. A year of work, of learning more of Jesus – of the Messiah. The people's feelings had grown sore. And his mother had died. Many Jews had left Jesus' open arms, and Malchus could feel the hate as strongly as if he could touch it. It wouldn't be long now.

The Messiah would be taken. Only yesterday he'd watched, palm leaf in hand with the others, as he'd arrived in Jerusalem on a donkey. He'd waved the palm leaf for only a brief moment, and watched as the Jews honored him with colored garments and tree limbs placed at his feet.

"Hosanna; Blessed is he that cometh in the name of the Messiah!" they'd shouted. "Blessed be the kingdom of our father David, that cometh in the name of the Messiah: Hosanna in the highest!"

The following day, Malchus found himself at the Nicanor Gate. The bleating of lambs and the smell of blood permeated the walls. But this was something Malchus had gotten used to, having guarded the area for many years. Also not surprising were those selling their merchandise and others trying, through the mob, to pay their temple tax, a yearly affair.

"Is it not written; my house shall be called of all nations the house of prayer? But ye have made it a den of thieves."

Unlike those who had just waved palm leaves for the Messiah, Jesus was suddenly casting out those who bought and sold in the Treasury with a reed of his own. With thunder, the table of the moneychangers was pushed over, and the money clanked and rolled near the table of doves, the chairs of the sellers tipping over with a crash. Those with recently purchased vessels could not carry them through the temple. Jesus would not allow it.

Malchus heard mumbling then, and raging anger, greater than any he'd heard before. The word "death" escaped the lips of more than one chief priest, and the scribes, ever willing to record the news, nodded their heads in agreement.

"But how will we destroy him?" one of them asked.

"By what authority doest thou these things? And who gave thee this authority?" came the question.

Malchus' fears were realized near the end of the week when Caiaphas called him into his private chambers. Caiaphas' palace was at the summit of a mountain that sloped down to a luscious garden. It was evening, and a slight breeze warmed Malchus' cheeks as he walked inside. The place was glorious. Like the kingdom of heaven on earth. Walls were overlaid with gold; pillars were carved with ornate birds and symbols of divine power. Only it wasn't power Malchus felt now, but danger.

"Hail!" Caiaphas began.

"Hail, most noble one."

"You were at the Temple Mount when Jesus destroyed the works of God?"

"Yes."

"Jesus. You know him?"

Malchus nodded.

"And his teachings?"

Again, Malchus nodded.

"It will happen tonight. Go with the others." He flicked his fingers toward the gilded door. "Meet with them at the Antonia Fortress."

"Yes, noble one." Malchus bowed once and stepped back without taking his eyes off the high priest until he'd reached the door. Guards on either side, eyed him casually before they opened the grand doors. They knew him just as he knew them.

Still, knowing the others – did little to assuage the grief that filled Malchus' heart.

The skies were obscured by clouds, and as Malchus gathered with the others, Judas, one of the disciples of the Messiah, stood within the throng. He would lead the way.

Approaching the garden, few spoke, but there were whispers of death and betrayal. They needed Judas so that the right person would be taken. The garden was dark as the group approached, although torches lit the evening sky. Judas was liked by most of the men who joined him, and the event would be a surprise.

The last thing Malchus wanted was to be there, but he'd been ordered, and orders must be followed. This Malchus had learned over and over again as a guard. He could not sleep when he needed to be awake. He must lead his men by example. He must always follow the instructions of Caiaphas. But his heart was heavy, and as the moment approached to take the Messiah, his eyes centered on him.

Judas, as planned, approached Jesus and kissed him on the cheek.

The shock was palatable to everyone it seemed, except the Messiah.

"Judas, betrayest the Son of man with a kiss?" Though he'd seen many disciples greet Rabbis with a kiss as a token of intimacy and respect, deep betrayal was in the air now.

Malchus moved to the front of the group. He would be one of the two to take him away.

"Messiah, shall we smite with the sword?"

He wasn't sure who had spoken. Might the apostles have swords? Had they been prepared for this very moment?

The pain came first, a deep penetrating pain. Seconds later, Malchus realized what had happened. He reached up, but only blood met his fingers. His ear had been severed and Jesus' eyes were on him. "Suffer ye thus far."

Malchus felt the Messiah's hand. Warmth surged through his ear. The blood that had dripped through his fingers just seconds before was now dry. And he beheld the Messiah. "Are you still listening?" Jesus whispered into his ear.

If he was listening, could he do this?

With faint awareness, Malchus took the Master to Caiaphas' house. He remembered one of his disciples crying bitterly outside. He remembered Jesus being struck and saying nothing. He remembered the jabs against his honor. The words of hate spewing from the lips of the men he had grown to honor.

He remembered the Messiah's eyes looking on him as if asking the question over and over: "Are you still listening?"

He thought of this question as Jesus was led to the hill of Calvary. He thought of it when he was nailed to the cross. When he cried out, "Father, forgive them; for they know not what they do." When the clouds darkened and rain fell and the earth shuddered in deep, whelping gasps. And he remembered the question at night when he finally managed sleep, in the house he had lived in with his mother and father.

Was he still listening? And if so, what was Jesus saying?

Four days after the crucifixion there was talk in the city that Jesus of Nazareth had risen from the dead. That he was amongst the people. That Mary had seen him and also the disciples.

With all of his heart, Malchus believed the words. He remembered them as he swept the house and readied it for the day just like his mother had done. He dressed for his day of work as Captain of the Temple guard; just like he had done many times before, walked to the door, opened it, and shut it behind him. He walked up the short path leading to the main road where travelers were often seen. But this time, he stopped.

Unlike days before, when the wind hissed and the trees uprooted themselves, and the ground rumbled; the skies were soft and the ground was firm.

"Follow thou me."

It was as if the words were spoken through the clouds.

Malchus bowed his head and wept.

He returned to his house, changed from his guard attire, and left it for the last time. It was early, but the disciples would be awake.

The Raising of Lazarus- -Sebastiano del Piombo, 1517 – 1519

The Raising of Lazarus
John 11

Martha lived in Bethany with her sister, Mary. Her brother, Lazarus, lived close by. Jesus visited them often when he was in Jerusalem.

The small village of Bethany was on the southeastern slopes of the city of Jerusalem, the Mount of Olives housed nearer the eastern slope. The dirt path from Bethany to Jerusalem was rocky and hilly. Little vegetation grew, though occasionally a pleasant plant of blue, red, purple, or white bloomed spontaneously, causing the traveler to stop and ponder, if only for a moment.

When Jesus was away, Martha would prepare the home for his coming reception; Mary would often walk the path in reflection. Often, she and her sister would speak together about the things they had learned. The home was cared for by both of them, though Martha had an affinity for household organization that couldn't be mistaken. Mary's love for the word of God brought many women to her door, asking questions, and receiving answers.

Like Jesus, Lazarus loved and respected each sister. With their focus on the home, he was often working in the fields. A farmer by trade, he found great joy in the planting and harvesting of olives for oil. There would be much to do between now and November, and Lazarus had hired many others to help him pick the olives that would then be pressed for oil. Olive oil was used for cooking and lamps primarily, but it had also been known to help in the healing of wounds.

Jesus had often visited both of their homes, and usually with fair warning, but not always, as he was wont to stop in and see how they were doing. They'd had such a day a few months before Lazarus became sick, a day to be remembered as Jesus taught them through the meal which consisted of bread, fruits – including figs and melon, pomegranates, and dates. Wine was offered, and fish, as well as olives for the few who liked the sour taste.

Martha had been upset that her sister listened at Jesus' feet while she worked in preparation for the feast. There were always many to feed; travelers that stopped by, friends and relatives who would join in the evening meal – including their brother, Lazarus.

It had been some time since they'd last seen Jesus, and Martha had volunteered to prepare this particular meal before the knowledge of Jesus' coming. On other days, it was Martha who heard the word of God and Mary who had been assigned the evening meal, though both were known to help one another with the task.

It was a grand occasion to sit at Jesus' feet, not only because he was the Master, but because women were never awarded such an opportunity at the feet of any teacher. Only men could be instructed in such a manner; as was their privilege. But Jesus treated women differently in this regard, as he did with most everything that he taught them.

On that day, as Jesus and his disciples had come unexpectedly, she had been counseled by Jesus not to worry about her sister listening at his feet. He had spoken to her so lovingly, so kindly. Still, he had charged her not to judge her sister. She had never forgotten his words, nor the character of her sister that had suddenly been revealed to her.

She loved her, not because they were the same, but because of their differences that brought them to Jesus, each, in turn, choosing the better part.

Life continued as usual after Jesus' visit, but it was never quite the same without him. There was time for cooking and bringing in guests, time for walking in the early morning hours and reflecting on the word of God, and time to hear his words at synagogue before his next visit; but his presence was sorely missed, though they knew his ministry was his calling.

As it was, the sickness of their brother started slowly enough. Sometimes he looked tired, and this just wasn't when he'd been working in the fields. He could be sitting or standing or working. When she noticed the blood coming as he coughed, he finally said something. He was sick and had been for months. Martha offered their home as a resting and healing place, and Lazarus had accepted. They were worried for him and offered more figs than usual during the morning and evening meals because figs were known to have medicinal value. Martha made a syrup of olive oil and Mary treated him at night, rubbing the liquid into his sore neck.

Physicians had been called. Prayers had been offered. But the day came Lazarus could not get out of bed.

It was nearing the end of March. The barley harvest would begin the following month, and, when complete, the Feast of the Passover of unleavened bread would begin. It was a joyous time of year, a time of celebration, and one Martha did not want her brother to miss. He was a good man, and through the years, had been stalwart and loving, filling their home with happiness.

A boy of fourteen, a cousin, was sent to fetch Jesus. Surely, Joel could find him and bring him back before it was too late. Two days later, Jesus was still not there, and their beloved brother was dead.

Martha grieved silently and as she watched Mary helping to ready the body, closing the eyes of their loved one and kissing his eyes with love, tears came from her own eyes. This, their brother was dead. Jesus could do all things. Why then, had he not come?

Words were spoken between them the next morning as they prepared the body, happy words of their brother's life and service, special prayers that his soul would reach heaven, but one question remained, at least in her mind. Why hadn't Jesus come? They would have to take him away now, and the two sisters would remain alone.

Mary washed his body with warm water and Martha anointed it with nard, myrrh, and aloe. Wrapping him in a shroud, his hands, and feet bound with strips of cloth, they covered his face with a linen napkin. The simplicity of the ritual had always eased Martha's mind, though this was the first time she had prepared a body to meet God.

Friends and relatives soon arrived. Many came, sharing their thoughts of the glorious resurrection – something Jesus had taught them on his visits to Jerusalem. Until Lazarus was buried, he wouldn't be left alone, even as most slept. She and Mary had decided that they would take turns throughout the night, as well as friends who had asked to sit with him to protect the body from harm.

Still, Jesus did not come.

The following morning, the body was carried out by male relatives and friends. The noise was great by those who followed behind: friends, loved ones, and neighbors joining the procession to the tomb. Flautists played. Occasionally, Mary and Martha stopped, and cried bitter tears, lamenting for all to hear.

At the tomb, the weeping was the most earnest. Martha reached for her sister's hand, and, as the body was carried into the family tomb, they wept in each other's arms.

Family and friends sat at the mourning enclosures – small seats made of earth and stone, in a row before the tomb, to express their final wishes. As the large stone was rolled over the opening, Martha's eyes turned to the sky.

Why hadn't Jesus come?

Every day, for four days after the burial, Martha returned to the tomb, as did Mary, at her own time and in her own way, to weep for the brother they loved. After seven days, ordinary life would somehow resume, and Martha would have to find someone else to tend to the fields. Many of their friends and relatives had come to comfort them during the week.

Where was he?

This she knew. If Jesus had been here, nothing, not even death, would have been possible. Her brother, *their* brother, would yet be alive. Leaving the sepulcher, Martha traveled up the road her brother Lazarus had known so well. The breeze was slight today, almost a caress, and as she walked beyond the town of Bethany, and to the places her brother had been fond of, especially the market, a familiar voice was heard.

"Aunt," he said, "I have found him!"

Martha turned. "Joel?"

"It is I. And Jesus, he is…"

Martha looked up. The form she knew. The eyes.

"Jesus!" she gasped, running to him; reaching for his hands. She must have looked a sight, walking in the afternoon heat, her hair wet from the baking sun, but nothing mattered now. "Lord," she began, "if thou hadst been here, my brother had not died. But I know, that even now, whatsoever thou wilt ask of God, God will give it thee."

"Thy brother shall rise again."

Her heart pounded at the words she knew were true. "I know he shall rise again in the resurrection at the last day."

"I am the resurrection, and the life: he that believeth in me, though he were dead, yet shall he live. And whosoever liveth and believeth in me shall never die. Believest thou this?"

"Yea, Lord: I believe that thou art the Christ, the Son of God, which should come into the world." These words she believed. These words she knew.

Turning from him for only a moment she thought of Mary still at the house.

"I must go to her!" she sang.

Traveling back the way she had come, her steps quick, her thoughts on what she would say, Martha found her way to the road, beyond the occasional wildflower, and to the house. Through the door she ran, stopping suddenly. A few friends had again gathered around her sister to comfort her.

"I must speak with thee," she whispered.

Into the kitchen, they walked. At once, Martha spoke: "The Master is come, and calleth for thee."

"The Master?"

Turning quickly, and preparing a shawl, Mary followed her sister beyond the tomb, down the road, and beyond Bethany, to the feet of Jesus, who was waiting for her.

Kneeling on the hard earth, she broached: "Lord, if thou hadst been here, my brother had not died." Others had followed her to Jesus, others she had not heard. She could hear them now, weeping, as she was.

"Where have ye laid him?" Jesus asked.

"Lord, come and see," the others answered.

Mary stood, and clasping the hand of her sister, turned to home. Jesus walked behind them, followed by the friends who'd been visiting with her sister, Mary. All were crying, even Jesus.

"Behold how he loved him!" someone said.

And surely, it was true.

"Could not this man, which opened the eyes of the blind, have caused that even this man should not have died?"

The striking words following the briefest words of love didn't surprise her. She had thought them herself, and recently too.

At the front of the sepulcher, they stopped. The great stone was still there, but the benches of stone placed for the burial had been removed. Tall trees surrounded them like a great hand. The sun was at its zenith, baring down on their faces, their hands, and feet. And yet, that didn't even matter – now.

"Take away the stone," Jesus said.

The request was surprising. Martha had thought the Lord would speak to them there, and share his love of Lazarus.

"Lord, by this time he stinketh: for he hath been dead four days," she whispered to him.

"Said I not unto thee, that, if thou wouldest believe, thou shouldest see the glory of God?"

Had he said so? *Yes.*

Martha looked on him, and with the help of many, the great stone was removed. All Martha could see was darkness. She turned to Jesus. His head was bowed. Moments that seemed like hours, lapsed as they waited. Finally, Jesus lifted his eyes to the heavens.

"Father," he said, "I thank thee that thou hast heard me. And I knew that thou hearest me always: but because of the people which stand by I said it, that they may believe that thou hast sent me."

And then, with a loud voice, Jesus spoke again: "Lazarus, come forth!"

It was only a moment, but again, Martha wondered at the words of Jesus until she saw the white shroud, and her brother, bound from head to foot, a linen napkin upon his face.

"Loose him, and let him go," Jesus said within the silence, for no one dared speak. It was like she was somewhere else, somewhere that spoke of love being the greatest of all gifts.

She reached for her brother, as did her sister, and, as they released him from their tight embrace, the linen upon his face fell to the earth.

The Centurion – James Tissot, 1886 – 1894

The Centurion

Mark 15

"What are you doing, Father?" the Centurion's son asked. He was seven.

"I am getting the crosses loaded," he replied.

"Who will die?" the boy asked.

The Centurion looked down at his son. He was a good boy, but he was always asking questions. And this question was harder than most.

"A couple of criminals," he replied. "And a man named Jesus."

"Jesus. I remember him."

"You do?"

"Why him, Father?"

The last cross thudded into the cart. It would be unloaded tomorrow, early at the Praetorium, ready as requested.

"There are many who do not believe the things he says," the Centurion told his son honestly.

"Do you, Father?"

The Centurion reached for his son. "Yes, I believe so," he said.

"Then you must do something, Father, you must save him."

Save him?

He was an officer currently stationed in Jerusalem and had eighty soldiers under his command. But his voice did not overshadow that of the chief priests. He was not above Pilate. Or even, the people.

No. This man the Jews called Jesus would soon be taking his last breath. And he could do nothing.

Barabbas, the criminal, had been chosen for release instead of the good man, the kind man, the man who'd healed his very own servant and caused the blind to see.

The morning came soon enough, it was clear and beautiful, and as he led Jesus into the Praetorium, the great hall, he thought again of the words of his son. He assigned one of his soldiers to clothe the man in purple as he watched. A crown of thorns was woven and pushed into his head by yet another. Jesus did not cry out.

He'd crucified many before Jesus. But not like this. Never – like this.

Jesus had been spat upon. Hit and whipped until the flesh of his back lay open in ribbons. And when a soldier under his command took the purple robe off of him, Jesus was pushed through the doorway; past the stable and the kitchen, to the central road where he would walk to his death.

"Hail, King of the Jews!" He had spouted the words along with the rest of them. Yelled them out as if he was nothing.

And he had worshiped him – mocked him – in order not to be singled out.

The cross-beam was heavy, too heavy. Even he – had struggled to unload it from the yard at the Praetorium.

The crowds were large. The yelling, the noise, ran through his ears. He could not think. He watched Jesus' feet. He watched him walk the road and its stone path, slick from many travelers. He watched his sandals, the back of his heels, the way he stepped – firmly. As if he hadn't been beaten, as if – he was a king.

The way was not flat. Stairs came and went, and people, so many people breathing and watching and speaking when they might have been silent. Tears. He saw the tears. The silence of some as they watched him. As he followed behind him.

Archways, so many archways above him. Like so many rising suns. The sheep gate. Dark tunnels, and windows with people peering from their depths. Watching – whispering about the man who would soon die. The path was narrow, like the minds of the people when it came to the teachings that they would not receive.

Jesus collapsed, the beam thudding to the ground. Everyone stopped. Voices halted. A man passed by. He knew the man and stopped him with his hand.

"Bear his cross," he demanded.

The man, Simon by name, the father of Tobias and Rufus, stopped.

"I have just left Cyrenaica," he said. "I am tired."

"Bear his cross."

The centurion knew the man to be thoughtful, if not a bit eccentric. And he was well-built; strong. He was tired, but he could carry the cross.

Simon pulled the beam to his shoulders, looking at him only once as he did so. His eyes had softened. A look came from the eyes of Jesus, a look the Centurion couldn't quite place. And then it came to him.

Years ago, when he was stationed in Capernaum. When his servant was sick. He could not work. And the Centurion had been in the marketplace, taking care of some skirmish he could no longer remember when he saw him.

"Lord, my servant lieth at home sick of the palsy, grievously tormented," he'd said, though others stood nearby, including some of the apostles.

Jesus had said to him, "I will come and heal him."

His heart had pounded. Jesus, in his home? "Lord, I am not worthy that thou shouldest come under my roof," he'd said. "But speak the word only, and my servant shall be healed. For I am a man under authority, having soldiers under me: and I say to this man, 'Go,' and he goeth; and to another, 'Come' and he cometh; and to my servant, 'Do this,' and he doeth it."

Jesus had watched him. He'd looked into his eyes. "Verily I say unto you, I have not found so great faith, no, not in Israel," he'd answered, placing a hand on his shoulder. His words as well as the gesture had surprised the Centurion.

"Many shall come from the east and west, and shall sit down with Abraham, and Isaac, and Jacob, in the kingdom of heaven. But the children of the kingdom shall be cast out into outer darkness: there shall be weeping and gnashing of teeth. Go thy way; and as thou hast believed, so be it done unto thee."

Finding a soldier to take his place, if only for a short time, he'd journeyed home only to find his wife crying.

"Come! Come!" she called to him, pulling him by his robe. He'd removed his helmet. His wood staff was laid quickly on the table. "Our servant is healed!" she continued. His children had looked on, their eyes wide and bright; the son of questions, and his two daughters – one and two years older, smiling widely.

The bed where the servant had lain for weeks and had writhed within was empty. Following his wife out to the stables, he'd met the servant amidst his duties, and they had spoken for a time.

"There is warmth in my heart. A Glowing," the servant had said as he touched his chest. "I am healed..."

The walk was slow, labored, and the voices only increased as Jesus made his way to Golgotha. The place of the skull.

The place frightened his children. His wife. And he – he was tired. It was his duty, and yet... The dark face in the rock above them threatened as he approached. Where evil resided, goodness would die. This was what he knew. The man named Jesus was good. Because of the miracle. No, because of the faith he'd offered before the miracle. Yes, and Jesus' power, these three had healed his servant.

Jesus was exhausted. The Centurion could hear his breath, shallow and labored, he could see the sweat dripping from his back. He could smell it.

And they were here, near the base of the hill, near where the people usually shopped for food or other goods. They were here for a purpose. To see Jesus crucified. Many looked afraid.

He had told his wife, his children, to stay home. It would not be good to see this. Even seeing the thieves would spin tales of death for months to come. He would not allow it.

They did not come.

But he was here. Here.

It was not his duty to drive the nails into Jesus' hands and feet. No. But he ordered it. He almost – felt it. He heard the tears, the laughter, the voices in prayer – in hate.

No, it would not be long now.

Jesus was lifted up.

The women cried at his feet. His mother. His friends. His apostles. The wailing broke through the clouds and continued to the heavens.

He could not breathe.

The superscription read: THE KING OF THE JEWS. Just like that. No one cared about the thieves hanging next to him. No one even looked. What they cared about was getting something to take home that Jesus had owned. His clothing. His robe. His sandals.

He wanted none of it.

But questioning eyes probed.

"Ah, thou that destroyest the temple, and buildest it in three days, save thyself, and come down from the cross," a man said, passing by the cross.

"He saved others; himself he cannot save," a chief priest mocked.

"Let Christ the King of Israel descend now from the cross, that we may see and believe," a woman spit.

"Save yourself, and us too," the thieves on either side chided.

Still, there was something in the air. Something that wrapped around Jesus that he could not see... He felt it. Something like... light.

Amidst the darkness, the thick darkness that was suddenly covering Golgotha, the Centurion felt it. It was the sixth hour, an hour not typical for darkness, and he was not afraid. Something had happened to him.

For three hours he stood in the darkness, feeling the light, and while others railed at Jesus, he felt only peace. At the ninth hour, Jesus spoke.

"My God, my God, why hast thou forsaken me?" The words whirled into the air and found a place inside the Centurion's heart.

Was Jesus forsaken?

He looked up at the skies. A single tear dripped down his cheek. His son's words echoed inside his soul, "You must do something, Father. You must save him."

"Behold, he calleth Elias," one of the women said.

A soldier ran, passing him quickly on the left. In his hand was a reed. "Let alone; let us see whether Elias will come to take him down," he said.

The Centurion knew what was in the reed. Wine and myrrh to deaden the pain. He also knew that Jesus would not take it. It was His time, and He would die.

For him.

For all of them.

Jesus cried out. His voice was loud. His head, once erect, fell to his chest.

A thunderous noise met his ears. The rain pelted his cheeks, washing away the lone tear that had stopped there. The ground heaved. Fear filled the skies as the women who loved him best held one other.

The Centurion was still standing. It was not like him to kneel on duty. He looked up again, searching the heavens.

"Truly this man was the Son of God." The words were spoken. They filled the air, his soul. He knew that God had heard him.

A soldier near him scoffed. He could hear his anger above the rain, the thunder, the shuddering of the ground. But the man's words of hate no longer mattered.

Only this.

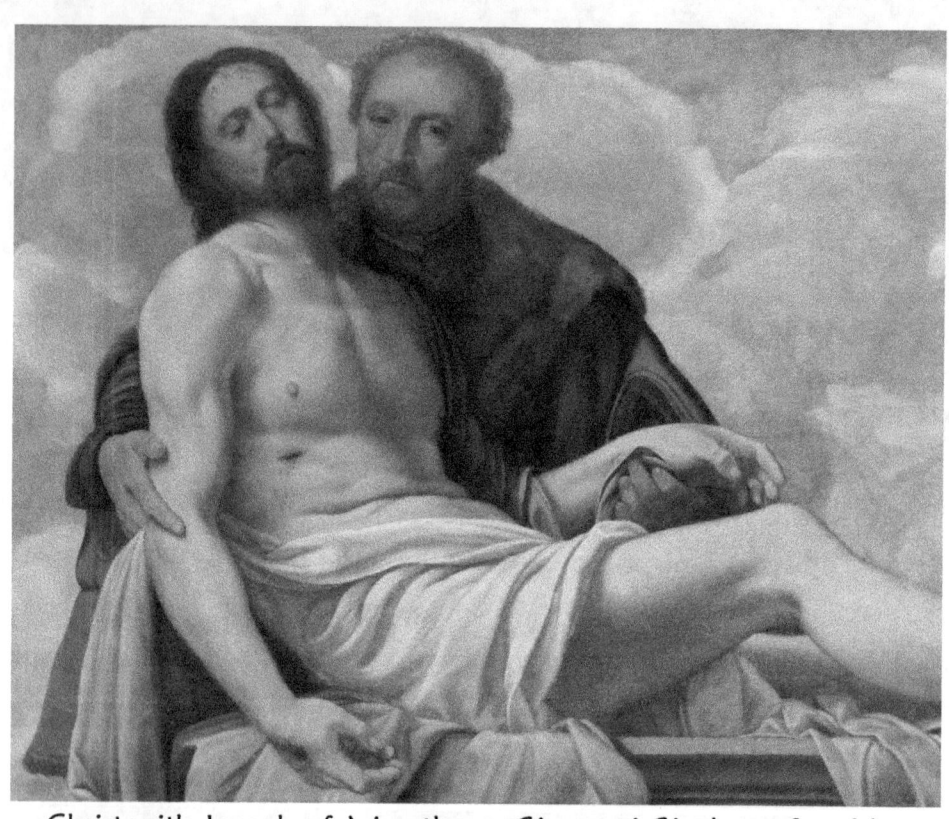

Christ with Joseph of Arimathea – Giovanni Girolamo Savoldo, 1525

The Sepulcher
Mark 15 & John 19

Joseph had been a member of the Sanhedrin for some years before Jesus's death. He was Jesus's great-uncle, uncle to Mary, and brother to Mary's mother. He had never lacked for anything in his life except the comfort his family may have given him if he'd chosen to live near them.

But as he'd grown, so had his desire to care for the people, especially his family, in the best way he knew how. Ruling in the Jewish law court was Joseph's profession. It paid well and allowed him luxuries many in his family could only dream about. He also controlled the tin trade for the Romans, allowing him many opportunities within their realm to view their concerns and misunderstandings, as well as to make friends with those more open to his voice.

In matters of faith, he was learning, but in the Law of the Jews, including Jewish manners, he was an expert. Even though he had rule over anyone who trespassed beyond the Court of the Gentiles along with The Council of Elders, he had no power beyond the administration of Jewish laws.

He hadn't returned to the upper Chamber of Hewn Stone just before the death of Jesus. He hadn't spoken with his colleagues. He hadn't taught. He had followed Jesus to his trial and the mount of crucifixion, had watched his death, along with many members of his family, and had returned home. Here, even the beauty of his surroundings could not comfort him. If he wished to talk with Jesus, council with him in precious matters of faith, he could no longer receive comfort.

For three years, since the beginning of his ministry to the people, Joseph had worried over him, but more recently the voices of the people had grown stronger against his authority. Trying to soften the hearts of others whom he daily dealt with had produced few results. Trying not to cross the line between sympathy and danger, was a daily concern. But now, now that his Lord and Savior was dead, he must cross the line.

As the skies had darkened, and just after the Centurion had pierced Jesus' side, and water and blood came rushing out, it had come to him. He must save the man whom it was said had saved him. He didn't understand it – not completely anyway. Discussions before his death on the cross had parted the cloud, but only for a moment. He was to take upon him the sins of the world. How was this to be done? The Lord never said, only that it would be done. He must have faith.

Reaching the Praetorium, previously built by Herod the Great and suited as Pilate's headquarters in the western part of the upper city, Joseph stopped at the grand doors. Two guards saluted him, and the doors were opened. In the courtyard of the great hall, he walked to the raised platform – Pilate's throne and judgment seat. It glittered in fine stones cemented in gold. There were others in the room, men and women speaking near him, but Joseph's full attention was on Pilate's red robe.

Upon his approach, the man smiled. "So, it is done," he said.

"I have come to thee secretly," was his response, trying to focus on the man who sat above him, his thick arms resting leisurely on the gilded armrests.

"The Jews?"

"They know not that I have come."

Pilot's smile narrowed. "For what is it that thou hast come?"

"To beg of you the body of Jesus."

"Of course." The man looked down on him airily.

As was the custom, Joseph looked down before meeting Pilate's eyes again. He had thought on having Nicodemus, his friend in Jewish tradition, though not always in faith, help him. But before he asked, he must get past Pilate.

"Where will he be buried?" Pilate asked.

"I have a sepulcher just beyond the place of crucifixion," was his reply.

"But what of you?"

"I do not need it. At least not now."

The man laughed. "Death may come to you sooner than you think."

Pilate was a man of his word, even in jest, and so Joseph remained silent as the man brooded, his thick beard and chin weighing heavily on his opened palm. When at last he looked up, his eyes glistened.

He turned to the Centurion that Joseph remembered had stood at the cross. He must have been summoned during their conversation, though Joseph had not known it.

"You are sure Jesus is dead?" he asked. "I don't want anyone saying he is resurrected when he is not."

The man bowed before Pilate. "Yes. He is dead. I watched his death myself."

Joseph might have been mistaken, but the Centurion, with his helmet off as he approached Pilate, looked thoughtful. Were those dried tears he saw through the sweat and dirt on his face?

Pilate stood, making his presence even more ominous. "See ye to it. It will give me one less thing to do." And flicking his fingers, he instructed the Centurion to take him to the place where Jesus was.

At the cross, they both stopped and looked up.

"I am glad you are taking him," the Centurion said. "He would have received much less from Pilate." Leaving Pilate's palace, he'd replaced his helmet, but his words penetrated Joseph's heart. "I have a friend; you know him as Nicodemus," Joseph said.

"Yes, I know the man. He is well respected in both the Jewish and Roman communities."

"Can you assist me now, and go for him later so that he might help me with the burial?"

"It is the least I can do."

"What is your name?"

"Claudius."

"You have a political heritage then."

"Yes. To the chagrin of my family I might have been a Roman of great position, but, instead, I was chosen out of many to do this." He looked up at Jesus and the two removed the body from the cross. A wagon was present. Jesus was laid inside.

"So, you do not like your profession?" Joseph asked.

The man hesitated. "Today, as I looked up at Jesus something happened to me. I think my profession will need to change."

There it was again. Something in the man's manner, his voice.

That night, after word arrived from Claudius to Nicodemus, he came to Jesus.

Nicodemus had to bend down slightly to enter the sepulcher, as Joseph had done just an hour before. He could tell that the rough-hewn walls of stone took his friend's breath away, but even more, the body of Jesus lying still on a slab jutting out from the rock.

There was no wind tonight. Only darkness. Only stillness. Joseph carried a lantern, as did his friend. The spices were ready and brought by Nicodemus. Myrrh and aloe. Together they wrapped Jesus in strips of linen. The sepulcher was in a beautiful spot within a garden, a place he'd chosen for his own burial many years before. But the sepulcher had never been meant for him, he knew that now.

He and his friend spoke little as the body was prepared. And once finished, they left the sepulcher.

"This is Claudius," Joseph said.

"I was surprised to see him," answered his friend, "but felt assured that it was so of what he spoke."

"And what did he speak?"

"I told him of one, Jesus, the Son of God, who was laid in a sepulcher, and that his friend, Joseph of Arimathea, wished to see him for the burial," Claudius said.

"You know him as the Son of God?" Nicodemus asked.

"Yes. My son. My little boy. We once had a servant healed in my home. I have always known the man was of God. Today, as Jesus was raised, I thought, my heart cannot hold this pain. And in a moment, it was gone."

Claudius removed his helmet. Tears were there.

"He is the Son of God and my life is His."

"Your life?" Nicodemus spoke, but his words were almost a whisper.

"My life, and the life of my son, and my wife, and later, perhaps those who serve within my home."

173

"What will you do?"

"I know not. But that doesn't matter, does it?"

He looked on Nicodemus and Nicodemus wiped at his cheek. "Perhaps... not."

The Pilgrims of Emmaus on the Road – James Tissot, 1886 – 1894

The Walk

Luke 24

Cleopas and Simeon had been friends since the beginning of time. As small boys, they had romped and played together in the village of Emmaus, about seven and a half miles from the city of Jerusalem. The stone path between the two places offered some shade through the forest for the weary traveler, but today the two friends hardly noticed the shade, their hearts heavy with grief.

The journey home, leaving Jerusalem just after sunrise, would take them roughly five hours, but the time spent together would be well-needed. They knew Jesus had been taken by the Roman soldiers; they also knew he'd been crucified and placed in a sepulcher. They had spoken with Mary. "He is gone," she'd said.

"How could Jesus be taken away?" Simeon asked his friend. He was older and wiser, for the most part, having spent many of his days hearing the words of Jesus, and studying his word. Two years made a big difference when one considered the Torah. At the age of two, when Simeon was still memorizing verses of the Torah, Cleopas had moved on to reciting the morning blessings, speaking grace following the meals, and doing good deeds.

"It was time that Jesus left us," answered Cleopas solemnly. "That could be the only reason."

"But he was young yet, not much older than we are."

Now that they were twenty and twenty-two, much had changed. Both were heavily engaged in *Midrash*, a form of teaching that involved questions and discussion about particular verses or sets of verses. What would often happen in this sort of exchange was what was legally called *Halakhah*, meaning 'to walk.' In other words, the walk opened the way for individuals to know what path to travel to please God. They knew in every detail how to obey the law with no derivation.

"But what of the stories taught by Jesus? What of his direction to improve one's life?" Simeon asked.

"You are referring to the *Aggadah*, of course."

"I don't care what it's called. I care what it does for me," Simeon answered, flicking up some dirt with his sandal. "This is how Jesus taught. He hated the oral tradition of the elders."

"Hate is a pretty strong word, brother."

"But didn't he say that a scribe which is instructed into the kingdom of heaven is like a householder which has treasure both old and new?

"The new oral tradition?"

"Yes. He told us that the scribes who practiced *Midrash* were disciples of the true master who brought forth old and new treasures."

But he also said: 'Why do ye also transgress the commandment of God by your tradition, because you forget to wash your hands before you eat'"?

"I guess it's a balance," said Simeon, stopping for a moment and looking into Cleopas's eyes. "I mean, Jesus told us the old laws – laws about the serpent and the bread of life – but he also spoke about specific subject matters – or *Mishnah* – and repeated to us the stories of God, expanding what we had learned as children."

"And older. I am going to miss that, brother."

They were silent for a moment as reflection gave way to speaking. And then Simeon asked, "What of the resurrection. What does it mean?"

"Jesus is no longer in the tomb. He has to be somewhere else."

"But where?"

Just then, footsteps were heard behind them. Looking back, Simeon said, "There's a man back there, walking alone."

"He has probably heard the news as we have," answered his brother. "Everyone has heard. Keep walking."

"Do you think someone has taken Jesus?" Simeon asked.

"Like who?"

"Maybe someone who hated him and wanted to cause trouble?"

"There are plenty of people like that. I don't think so," Cleopas answered quietly.

"Then he has been resurrected as the women said."

"Which brings us to the same question," offered Cleopas. "Where is he?"

The man behind them had caught up and now walked at the side of Simeon. "What manner of communications are these that ye have one to another, as ye walk, and are sad?"

"Art thou only a stranger in Jerusalem, and hast not known the things which are come to pass there in these days?" Simeon asked.

"What things?"

The man seemed earnest to both brothers. Truly, he hadn't heard what had happened to the Master they reasoned.

"Concerning Jesus of Nazareth, which was a prophet mighty in deed and word before God and all the people," began Cleopas.

"And how the chief priests and our rulers delivered him to be condemned to death, and have crucified him. But we trusted that it had been he which should have redeemed Israel," continued Simeon.

"And be side all this," Cleopas added, "to day is the third day since these things were done. Yea, and certain women also of our company made us astonished, which were early at the sepulcher; and when they found not his body, they came, saying, 'We have also seen a vision of angels, which said he was alive.' And certain of them which were with us went to the sepulcher, and found it even so as the women had said: but they saw him not."

The man spoke, and Cleopas suddenly wondered if he was a prophet: "O ye unwise, and slow of heart to believe all that the prophets have spoken: Ought not Christ to have suffered these things, and to enter into his glory? Remember Moses, and all the prophets after him, who have testified of Christ? Remember Isaiah's words? 'He is despised and rejected of men, a man of sorrows, and acquainted with grief: and we hid as it were our faces from him; he was despised, and we esteemed him not. Surely he hath borne our griefs, and carried out sorrows: yet we did esteem him stricken, smitten of God, and afflicted. But he was wounded for our transgressions, he was bruised for our iniquities: the chastisement of our peace was upon him; and with his stripes we are healed.'"

"Remember the words of the apostles? Their words of comfort? 'It behooved Christ to suffer, and to rise from the dead the third day' The words of the women that you have heard with your own ears? 'He is not here: for he is risen'?

Rememberest thou this?"

Both brothers nodded.

And even Jesus himself hath said, "Therefore doth my Father love me, because I lay down my life, that I might take it again").

Again, the brothers remembered. But they could not speak.

As they drew near their village, the man grew quiet and turned as if to leave them. They were almost home and their time had been well-spent, still, the thought of him leaving them created greater sadness than they had first experienced before he'd spoken with them.

"Abide with us: for it is toward [noon], and the day is far spent," Cleopas offered. The man looked down at Simeon as if requesting an answer.

"Please," he said.

And so, the man followed.

They walked beyond the thick trees that gave entrance to their village, through the narrow pathway, near the well, and beyond a few homes made of thatch and stone. Like others in the village, their home was simply constructed but well kept. Once there, they would serve the bread and wine, and produce the grapes and figs picked just two days prior. And they would talk about Jesus.

Once the food was placed on the table, the man took a piece of the bread, blessed it, break it, and gave it to them. The singularity of the moment struck both brothers with wondering awe. Who else could break bread like this but Jesus himself?

And then, just as suddenly he was gone.

When they dared speak, Simeon spoke first. "Was it he?"

"Did not your heart burn within you, while he talked with us by the way, and while he opened unto us the scriptures?" Cleopas asked.

"But why us?"

"We are his disciples."

"Yes, but we are of the very least."

"I know. But having him come – having him join us – that has to mean something. But what?"

181

Simeon wiped at his cheek. A tear had fallen there. He could smell the bread, still sitting on the plate where Jesus had broken it. He could smell the wine in the cups. The figs and grapes were laid out in front of them. No one had touched the fruit. But Jesus had touched the bread. "It means, Jesus has been resurrected as he has said. He is the bread of life. We must return."

That very hour, the brothers returned to Jerusalem, thinking how Jesus had come to them. What he'd spoken about, and what he'd done – after he'd entered their home. The eleven were gathered together and their wives and children. The time was just before sunset.

As they sat together, speaking about the risen Lord and what things were done on the way to their home, and how he was known of them in breaking of bread, Jesus stood in the midst.

"Peace be unto you."

Simeon was afraid. Had a spirit appeared unto them? He and Cleopas were silent. No one spoke, not even the children.

"Why are ye troubled? Why do thoughts arise in your hearts? Behold my hands and my feet, that it is I myself: handle me, and see; for a spirit hath not flesh and bones, as ye see me have."

Jesus opened his hands and spread his fingers so that they could see. Simeon did see. He saw the marks – the crucifixion marks – on his hands and feet. Cleopas also saw, and the disciples, the mothers, and the children. In time, all had stood from the supper table – all had felt the wounds.

Jesus?

"Have ye here any meat?"

Jesus turned to the table and sat, looking at each one of them in turn, stopping finally to look at his mother.

She was crying. "We have broiled fish and honeycomb," she said.

"Thank you, Mother."

Cleopas would speak to Simeon later about the thoughts he'd had the evening of Jesus's resurrection when the eyes of his understanding were opened. And Simeon would speak to Cleopas about his new understanding – he would share his testimony about the risen Lord, and the great joy he felt that he had seen him, but there were things they never shared. Truths spoken by Jesus on the eve of the resurrection, sacred words, meant only to their mind and heart. Truths that came from God.

St. John the Evangelist – Vladimir Borovikovsky, 1804

Salome's Wish

Doctrine & Covenants 7

Salome was known amongst the followers of Jesus. She was the mother of James and John, the wife of Zebedee, a woman of faith, a sister of Mary – if only in the gospel. But she preferred standing in the shadows, helping the twelve and Jesus where needed, keeping to herself.

It wasn't that Salome didn't know the truth; she just couldn't express it like the others.

Her sister, Mary, had never stopped caring for her, even after she married Joseph, and Jesus had been born followed by James, Joses, Simon, Judas, Mary, Elizabeth, and Eve. Jesus's father, Joseph, had died just a few years before Jesus's ministry.

Mary Magdalene, who had once housed within her soul seven devils, had been her friend since her healing at the beginning of the Master's ministry. Mary Magdalene never cared that her friend's speech was slow, and as often as she could, they would talk together about her new life.

Salome's speech had never been perfect. And the others – they had always been kind to her – had always included her, though, with the Master, it was different. He always sought her out, gave occasion to speak to her when she was cooking a meal or caring for the lambs.

He always knew when she was sad, when she was encumbered, and when she needed someone to listen to her.

He spoke only of her. How she was doing. What she needed. Only once in the many years she'd known him, had he spoken of himself.

"I am the way," he told her. "I am the resurrection and the life. Follow after me and ye shall never hunger, ye shall never thirst."

"How do I – follow?" she asked.

Touching her hand, he smiled.

"Come with me as I travel. Listen to my words. Believe. Zebedee needs you. Your children need you."

"*My* sons of thunder?" she asked.

He laughed. "Yes. They love you."

Her sons. They weren't easy to forget. She would turn her back and James would be drinking from the water jug, her son, John, right behind him, spilling the olives and figs for supper all over her newly washed floor. As they'd grown up, it was always one hiding from the other, or both of them hiding from their parents.

In the gospel, they were eager learners, always waiting to out-best the other; in daily life, it was the same. Only a year apart in age, they learned from the Torah, spoke at synagogue, and gave themselves to mighty prayer. They had followed Jesus, and she and her husband and sons had been near as the Master had healed and blessed. She would never forget the feelings within her heart as she watched the daughter of Jairus come to the door, and walk amongst her neighbors and friends – brought back from death.

She would never forget all she had heard and seen. She couldn't.

Neither could she forget the day her sons returned from the mount.

Their hair glistened like the sun, and their eyes, usually a warm brown, glinted amber in their depths. They had never been so silent, so reflective. And while James spoke to her of the glowing garments of Jesus and of going to heaven when the time came, John spoke of something else entirely.

He was not to die at all.

"Mother, it was remarkable. I am to live until the Master comes again at the end of time."

She was awestruck.

What did her son mean?

"I shall see all things, Mother. All things."

"John, my beloved," he said unto me, "what desirest thou? For if ye shall ask what you will, it will be granted unto you." They were sitting at the table. It was night. Supper had been served and cleared. All others had made their way to the roof where it was cooler.

And I said, "Lord, give me power over death, that I may live and bring souls unto thee."

And the Lord said, "Verily, verily I say unto thee, because thou desirest this thou shalt tarry until I come in my glory, and shalt prophesy before nations, kindreds, tongues, and people."

"My son." She reached for him then, touching the warm hand that had held her own as a young boy. "My son."

She touched his hair. "And – the Master?" she asked.

"As I said at supper, he has returned to Father."

"That's – right."

"Do not worry over me, Mother. I feel changed. I feel as if I will be able to do all things now whatsoever the spirit listeth."

She turned away from her son, and with her long sleeve, wiped at her eyes. It was marvelous, the words of her son. And James?

He seemed to read her thoughts.

"My brother will stay here until death as Jesus has said. After death, he will go speedily to God's kingdom."

She was silent after that, silent as he stood, and silent as he left her to gather with the family on the roof. He turned before leaving the room. "Are you coming?" he asked.

"In a moment..."

Many years had passed since that day, and Salome wondered where her son was now. She knew of his duties as a teacher and as a healer. In the years before his banishment to Patmos, he had healed, taught, and loved. But he was gone now, as was James, beheaded by Herod. The Master had suffered and died for them all. He'd appeared to many. His time in Gethsemane was long past, but the feeling in her heart remained unchanged.

And she was old.

Her speech had not improved with age. If anything, her halting words were even more pronounced. Others found it difficult to understand her. Most of her family were older now too, many were dead, including her beloved husband, Zebedee.

But the warmth in her heart had not ceased since her last visit with Jesus before his resurrection. Along with Mary Magdalene, and Mary, the mother of Jesus, she had been asked to bring the sweet spices to anoint the Master. This she had done with quietness and respect. And as they mourned and wept over him, their lamps lit in the darkness, she had thought again of his words to her.

"I am the resurrection and the life. Follow after me and ye shall never hunger, ye shall never thirst."

She had believed him then. And she believed him now – today, as she sat alone in the beautiful home constructed by her husband for her pleasure. It was large and she was alone.

And yet...

That feeling, she could not mistake it.

"Y-yes?" she asked.

She could not see him, but just a touch and she would know for sure.

There.

"You are finally here," she said.

She turned. John stood before her.

He took her hand. "It is time," he said.

"You look so young."

He smiled, a small tear falling from his right cheek. "You have outlived most of the family," he said.

"Except for you."

"I have many, many years ahead of me," he said.

"What do you think it will be like?" she asked.

"About the same as now," he answered, touching her gray hair and looking deeply into her eyes. "Except, I have a feeling that just won't leave me. The life I live will see many changes. And there shall be a temple built upon the mountains. It shall be far away from here. And the people who love the Lord will be taught there, and great shall be their peace."

"You sound like the prophet Isaiah," she said.

"I have been thinking about him a lot as of late," he answered. "There are many things I've thought about, including you."

He hugged her.

"Now, you must go. He is waiting."

But she had a question. A question that could no longer wait. And just as before, as the many years that had come and gone had vanished behind her, she still could not ask it, the question yet filling her heart.

"I know your wish," her son said, holding her close. "Can't you hear it?"

She blinked up at him. She did not know what he meant. Her voice. It had always been about her voice. The lack of proper language had always gotten in the way. She had never been able to speak her heart, share her testimony of the Master without stalling for the right words. She would never be able to speak in a way that others would truly listen.

He laughed. "Oh, Mother," he said. "You don't hear it?"

"I don't hear anything but your laughter," she said. "No one knows my heart, the words I desire to speak, all the years I have felt God in my life with no one to hear and understand, except for Him."

"How about now?" He was still grinning down at her.

"Now?"

"You are speaking fully. You are not halting between words."

"I'm not?"

"Listen to yourself. Are you doubting what you hear?"

He touched her cheek. "Oh, Mother, I love you so."

"I love you, too. How long before I die?"

"Soon." He paused, and pulled her back from him, looking again into her eyes. "Don't you realize, Mother, what plans the Lord has for you? Have you forgotten the testimony that you have forever given to others with your eyes?"

"My eyes?"

"Of course."

"My brother and I were always getting into everything, competing for your attention, trying to outmaneuver the other. And you always knew what to say. Your eyes, the way you lived and still do, testify of your love of the gospel. Isn't it so?"

"But I had so much to say, to tell you!"

"And you have. When I go about teaching God's followers until the end of time, when I reach out to someone who has fallen to the earth because they feel as if hope is gone, as I am preaching to the multitudes or the one about the love of God and His plan for them, I will remember your eyes, Mother. I will remember your eyes and what they said to me."

"Oh, my son!"

She could hear it now, the sound of her voice, clear, like the waters of Galilee. She could feel the change like the day John came to her and spoke to her about him living on the earth until the Master's second coming.

Inside her son's amber eyes – was love.

Citations

(1)   *Page 28: Give Me This Water That I Thirst Not: The Woman at the well*, Camille Fronk (https://womensconference.ce.byu.edu/sites/womensconference.ce.byu.edu/files/fronk_camille_0.pdf), 2000.

(2)   Page 55: (see Shema and the Tephilla, Jewish prayers; Deut. 6:4-7; Mark 12:26; Matt. 11:25)

(3)   *Page 132: Jerusalem – The Eternal City*, David B. Galbraith, D. Kelly Ogden, Andrew C. Skinner, page 190.

Dear Reader,

Enjoy this book? Did it change the way you think or lend voice to new thoughts about Jesus or the least of these? Please share your thoughts in a review on Amazon. I would appreciate it.

Have a beautiful day!

Kathryn

Check out my other books: t.ly/7BDR

Scripture References in Dialogue

Pages 103-111 – John 9:1-41

Page 103 – John 8:47

Pages 118-119 – John 6:1-13

Page 123 – Luke 2:48-49

Pages 125-128 – John 7: 15-20, 25-52

Pages 129- 130 – John 8: 3-11

Pages 130-131 – John 8:12-32

Page 133 – Mark 11: 9-10

Page 134 – Mark 11:15-19

Page 136 – Luke 22:47-51

Page 136 – Luke 23:34

Page 143-146 – John 11:21-44

Page 149 – Mark 15:18

Page 150 – Mark 15:21

Page 151 – Matthew 8:6-13

Page 152-154 – Mark 15:25-39

Page 158 – Matthew 27:58

Page 164 – Matthew 13:52, Matthew 15:2-3

Page 165-168 – Luke 17-43, Luke 24:18-27

Page 166 –Isaiah 53:2-5, Luke 24:46, Matthew 28:6

Page 173 – D&C 3:1-3

Picture Index

"Figure of Christ" – Heinrich Hofmann, 1884 - Heinrich Hofmann, Public domain, via Wikimedia Commons

"Nicodemus and Jesus" - Alexandre Bida, 1874 - Alexander Bida, Public domain, via Wikimedia Commons

"Christus und die Samariterin am Brunnen" - Angelika Kauffmann, 1796, Angelica Kauffmann, Public domain, via Wikimedia Commons

"The Woman with an Issue of Blood" – James Tissot, 1886-1896, James Tissot, Public domain, via Wikimedia Commons

Christ sits at the bedside of Jairus's sickening daughter - Etching by E.F. Mohn after G.C. von Max, 1840-1915, Wellcome Collection

"Raising the Young Man of Nain" – Paolo Veronese, 1560s, Paolo Veronese, Public domain, via Wikimedia Commons

"Jesus Anointing" – Alexander Bida, 1874, Alexander Bida, Public domain, via Wikimedia Commons

"The Palsied Man Let Down through the Roof" – James Tissot, 1886*1896, James Tissot, Public domain, via Wikimedia Commons

"The Blind and Mute Man Possessed by Devils" – James Tissot, 1886 – 1894, James Tissot, Public domain, via Wikimedia Commons

"The Healing of the Ten Lepers" – James Tissot, 1886-1894, James Tissot, Public domain, via Wikimedia Commons

"The Blind Man at the Pool of Siloam" – Edmund Blair Leighton, 1879. Ben P L, Public domain, via Wikimedia Commons

"The Miracle of the Loaves and the Fishes" – Bartolome EstebanMurillo, 1617 – 1682, Bartolomé Esteban Murillo, Public domain, via Wikimedia Commons

"Christ Healing the Ear of Malchus" – Louis Finson, 1600 – 1630. Circle of Louis Finson, Public domain, via Wikimedia Commons

"The Raising of Lazarus"- -Sebastiano del Piombo, 1517 – 1519, Sebastiano del Piombo, Public domain, via Wikimedia Commons

"The Centurion" – James Tissot, 1886 – 1894, James Tissot, Public domain, via Wikimedia Commons

"Christ with Joseph of Arimathea" – Giovanni Girolamo Savoldo, 1525, Girolamo Savoldo, Public domain, via Wikimedia Commons

"The Pilgrims of Emmaus on the Road" – James Tissot, 1886 – 1894, James Tissot, Public domain, via Wikimedia Commons

"St. John the Evangelist" – Vladimir Borovikovsky, 1804, Vladimir Borovikovsky, Public domain, via Wikimedia Commons

www.ingramcontent.com/pod-product-compliance
Lightning Source LLC
Chambersburg PA
CBHW070749180626
46818CB00007B/3046